THE MISS HEREFORD STORIES

The
Miss Hereford
Stories

GAIL
ANDERSON-DARGATZ

To Elizabeth

Wmy Thanks for

everything

Gail Anderson-Dargatz!

Douglas & McIntyre
Vancouver/Toronto

94 95 96 97 98   5 4 3 2 1

Douglas & McIntyre
1615 Venables Street
Vancouver, British Columbia
V5L 2H1

Canadian Cataloguing in Publication Data

Anderson-Dargatz, Gail, 1963-
The Miss Hereford stories

ISBN 1-55054-160-9

I. Title.
PS8551.N42M5 1994   C813.'54   C94-910464-7
PR9199.3.A52M5 1994

Editing by Barbara Pulling
Cover illustration by Franklin Hammond
Cover and text design by Michael Solomon
Typeset by Compeer Typographic Services Ltd.
Printed and bound in Canada by Webcom Ltd.
Printed on acid-free paper ∞

All characters in *The Miss Hereford Stories* are entirely
fictional. Any resemblance they may bear to real
persons and experiences is illusory.

Navel Gazing was published in slightly different form
in *Canadian Author*.
Quotations are taken from the *Holy Bible*, New
American Standard Translation, placed by the Gideons.

The publisher gratefully acknowledges the assistance of
the Canada Council and the British Columbia
Ministry of Tourism, Small Business and Culture for
its publishing programs.

To Cowboy Floyd and Cow M19—
Putting on that cow suit was
the best thing I ever did

CONTENTS

MISS HEREFORD

THE Miss Hereford contest was no big deal for a town the size of Camrose where, rumour had it, Doris Day had been born. But for the town of Likely, the first Miss Hereford competition, in 1969, was an event. Likely is what you call a half-horse town; we had no newspaper, the coffee shop was "the Cafe," the hotel was "the Hotel" and the tavern was "the Tavern." If you wanted fancy you went to Camrose.

The Hereford Breeders' Club timed the Miss Hereford contest to take place just before the 4-H shows at the Likely Fall Fair. It took the urging of Wallace Hammerstein, the only tractor and hardware dealer in Likely, to get the Hereford Club members even considering the idea. I know, I was there, sitting on a kid's wooden chair, trying to hold in a fart.

Kids weren't allowed at important meetings like this, so me being there was a big deal, and an oversight by my parents, who'd forgotten I was in the back of the pickup. They'd just taken me into Camrose to see the doctor. While helping my dad milk that morning, I'd stuck one of the milking inflations — the cup that fits over the cow's teat and sucks the milk from her — on my forehead. I don't know why. In any case, the sucking action of the milk inflation left a hickey on my forehead. That was the first time I'd heard the word "hickey." The doctor looked at the mark, shook his head, and slapped a bandage on it. Once there was nothing more to be done, my parents left me in the back of the pickup in the Safeway parking lot and did some grocery shopping. They then realized they were late for the Hereford Club meeting and, with me still stretched out on a pile of hay in the back of the truck, sped back to Likely. From guilt at forgetting me, and as it had begun to rain, they were forced to take me and my hickied forehead inside. "Don't say a word," my mother told me.

"What happened to Martin?" said Mrs. Shute.

"A scratch," said my mother.

Mrs. Julie Shute was the Hereford Breeders' Club secretary, although she'd never raised a Hereford in her life. Mrs. Hammerstein said Mrs. Shute had only joined the club to meet men. Mrs. Shute was my accordion teacher and the mother of my best friend, Nevil Shute. She was a town lady, tall and fashionable by Likely standards, who wore matching two-piece Jackie Kennedy suits that were only five years out of date. She frightened everyone because she was the only woman in Likely who worked at an outside job. She was a bank teller in Camrose, a job she'd taken on after her husband died of a heart attack. He'd been a banker, a loan's officer, and had also been called Nevil. Neither Nevil Shute was any relation to the author, although to avoid confusion we took to calling my friend "Likely Nevil" as he got older. Mrs. Shute crammed the craziest stuff into every nook and cranny of her house, like the porcupine skull in the dish cupboard, the collection of antique toasters in the music room, and the little glass ball she kept on the fireplace mantel that Mrs. Hammerstein said Mrs. Shute used for fortune telling and other witch things.

That was the other side of Mrs. Shute. She was rumoured to sell medicinal preparations she concocted herself, and she sometimes accepted gifts of beef and pork in payment for counselling warring couples or negotiating land sales. My mother said Mrs. Shute was *Ukrainian*, as if that explained it all. Mrs. Shute's mother, Mrs. Zachariuk, had been a midwife in the early days of Likely. My mother said Mrs. Zachariuk had the uncanny talent of telling the sex of a child while the baby was still in the womb, just by laying her hands on the mother's belly. It was a skill Mrs. Shute inherited. Around the time of the Miss Hereford contest, Mrs. Shute taught herself belly dancing in her two-piece bathing suit in front of her living room window to a record called "Learn Belly Dancing in Your Own Home" she got through a mail order ad. That turned some people against her, but generally her counsel was sought after. Pastor Gottlieb, of course, didn't like it one bit.

The Hereford Club always met in the only place big enough, the basement of the old dance hall that was currently Lamentations Church. Wallace Hammerstein, who owned the building, rented it out to the church for a respectable sum. The irony — that the Lamentations brethren, a tiny offshoot Baptist sect, were now taking communion in a dance hall — was not lost on any of us. "We'll roll the devil right out of these boards," Pastor Gottlieb had said as he rolled Bjarne Lindskoog's old stock tank, now resurrected as our baptismal tank, up to the front of the hall near the pulpit. Our minister himself was a recent acquisition. Pastor Gottlieb had been a Hereford breeder in Likely until just seven years before, when he received the call. As a consequence, we got a lot of sermons based on the behaviour of cattle, on how we were not animals; we were destined for a place above the angels, in fact, once we were dead, and we should act like it.

The Herefords' meeting room opened up into the kitchen so that the women could keep the coffee perking and cookie plates filled, and still listen in. Mom brought me a glass of juice and one of Mrs. Hammerstein's brownies, brushed hay off my jack-shirt, and told me to be a good boy and stop picking my nose.

The idea was for the Miss Hereford contestants to go out and sell raffle tickets on a prize Hereford calf. Whoever sold the most tickets would be crowned Miss Hereford. Of course the contestants also had to make a speech on Herefords and wear pretty dresses.

Dad said, "I don't like the idea."

"The contest's upped membership in every club that's held one," said Hammerstein.

"Good promotion," said Rudy Bierlie, crossing his fake leg over his real one. Mr. Bierlie was the high school shop instructor. His fake leg replaced the one he had lost to a threshing machine. He also taught courses in farm safety; when he talked safety, folks listened. "Get involved, and you stand to get your names known," said Mr. Bierlie. "That's a fact."

"Good experience for the girls," said Hammerstein.

"Good experience?" said Mrs. Shute. "It's a bleeping popularity contest."

"Not even that," said Bjarne Lindskoog. "It's which girl's folks got the most bucks, so they can buy the most tickets."

Bjarne Lindskoog was my 4-H club leader, and I knew what he was talking about. Hammerstein's daughter, Gudrun, was in the same grade as my sister, Louise, grade 11, and even I guessed that Gudrun first came up with the idea of the Miss Hereford contest. Gudrun was loud and she got good grades. Louise called her uncouth. I went to school with her kid brother, Wallace Junior, who pushed me into mud puddles and wiped snot on his sleeve.

"I've seen pictures," said my mother. "They wear lipstick."

"That's not so bad," said Hammerstein. "I let my girl wear lipstick."

His wife wore lipstick, too, but that's all she or Gudrun wore for make-up. Neither of them got much sun and they were white like pastry lard. When you saw them walking, all you saw were lips, bellies and bird legs. Wallace Hammerstein, on the other hand, had the poise and manner of a buffalo.

"Doesn't seem fitting to parade young girls on a stage," said Dad.

"Like they were harlots," said my mother.

My father put a warning hand on my mother's arm. "Now, it's not that bad," he said.

"There won't be any parading around in bathing suits," said Mr. Bierlie.

"Of course not," said Hammerstein.

"We'll teach the girls social graces," said Mrs. Hammerstein. "How to talk proper, good posture, give speeches."

"Yah, they get that from 4-H," said Bjarne Lindskoog.

"It's not a beauty contest," said Mr. Bierlie. "The girl who wins will have to know about Herefords and giving speeches. That's what the whole thing's about."

"So it would be like a 4-H speech competition?" said Mom.

"Exactly," said Rudy. "Nothing different from that. It's just the girl who wins goes around to all the fairs and promotes our club. She'll get all kinds of folks interested in our Herefords. There's a whole untapped market out there."

"Well, I can't see how that would hurt anything," said Dad.

"And no one's going to force any girl to do anything she doesn't want to," said Wallace. "No one's saying you'd have to enter your girl."

"I don't know," said Mom.

"I guess it's all a little new," said Dad. "I'm sure we'll get used to the idea."

"It's really for older 4-H girls," said Hammerstein. "It'll be a chance for them to end their time in the club with a bang."

"Like Louise," said my father and patted my mother's arm.

"Oh, no," said my mother. "No, no, no."

"Just kidding," said my father.

When we got home that night, we talked about the Hereford meeting over hot chocolate and apple strudel in my mother's kitchen. Louise was in a foul mood, maybe because Mom had told her to get off the phone when we walked in. I said to Louise, "Don't you want to be Miss Hereford?" and put my fingers at my head like horns and wiggled my hips across the kitchen floor. Louise said, "Idiot." Sometimes she made out like she was too grown up to let her idiot brother bug her. Other times it worked.

"You wouldn't win anyway," I said. "Too ugly."

"Martin," said my mother.

"You little creep," said Louise, and she hit me across the head, except I guess she forgot she still had her strudel in her hand and she got me in the eye with it. I wiped it off and licked my fingers. You have to understand Louise wasn't all that ugly — plenty of guys would've asked her out if she wasn't so mean-mouthed — but she thought she was. She had curly red hair to her shoulders and a classic hourglass figure, but Mom made her wear gorky clothes, like the bobby socks and ankle-length skirt she had on that night, and tie her hair up in a bun. In fact, dressed like that, she was the spitting image of my mother in that photograph on the piano taken in 1953. I pulled at the sleeve of Louise's cardigan and she pulled it back so it stretched all out of shape.

"Little fart," she said. "Leave me alone."

"Louise!" said my mother. My mother had grown up believing the word "fart" was as bad as that other "F" word, and I sometimes said "beef heart, beef heart" really fast, just to taunt her.

"Miss Hereford," said Louise. "Prettiest cow. Bet Gudrun Hammerstein wins."

"Louise!" said my mother. I got a kick out of this because Mom hardly ever yelled at Louise. "You will not talk about people that way."

"She's a cow," said Louise. Louise never talked like that around Mom or Dad, only with her friends at the Cafe after school. Then I thought maybe it wasn't Shirley Clapstein on the phone like she said; maybe it was Russell Schmidt, the guy who asked Louise to the movie and Mom said no. "Gudrun knows she's the only one who'd enter," said Louise, "and the only one who'd win. Everybody'd vote for her, and get a deal on equipment from her dad."

"That's not the way it is!" said my mother. "This is a Hereford Association pageant. Your father and I have been members for twenty years. We'd have no part if there were any shady dealings."

My father raised his index finger. "But the lipstick," he said.

"Never mind about the lipstick," said my mother.

"It's a farce," said Louise. "It's who can buy the honour of being Miss Hereford. Now that's a laugh. Miss Hereford. What an honour. Moooo."

Louise was unwise to wound my mother's pride. In a

community where raising the best darn Hereford cow and baking the sweetest squares were life's only sanctioned pleasures, pride wasn't a sin, it was a necessity. My mother was a proud member of the Likely Hereford Breeders' Club, and its willing defender.

"You'd learn a thing or two by entering that contest, young lady," said my mother.

"Yeah," said Louise. "Like how to chew my cud with my mouth closed, and how to shoo those pesky flies away while maintaining poise."

"You'd learn about community, young lady, and about working for a worthy cause. You'd learn how to make speeches and act like a lady. It appears you need some help in that area."

Me and Dad, we were looking from Louise to Mom, from Mom to Louise; this was better than slipping down to the General Store to watch the hockey game when Mom thought we were out cleaning the calf stalls. That is, until Mom stiffened and looked us both down. "Don't you have cows to feed?" she said, and her voice was tight, like we should go do chores whether we had to or not. Even though it was only the first week of school and not what you'd call cold outside, Dad and me took our time, scrounging around in the hallway closet for our jack-shirts, rubber boots and the brown toques that Mom had made the winter before, getting in as much of this dispute as we could. Just before Dad slammed the door behind us, I heard Mom say, "Young lady, you're entering that contest whether you want to or not."

Louise didn't go quietly. "This is stupid," she said as she picked up a stack of old issues of the *Hereford Digest*. "I don't believe this," she said as she walked across the kitchen floor with the *Fanny Farmer Cookbook* on her head. And, as she posed in the basement of Lamentations Church for the

Leduc Representative photographer, she said, "Moo." After that, my sister was known around Likely as "the one with the lips."

I guess it wasn't too surprising that when Louise got away from the house and was on her own turf, say at school or the Cafe, she went crazy. Sometimes she got Shirley Clapstein to lend her clothes and changed in the girls' washroom at school. She wore jeans and T-shirts — clothes Mom would never buy her — let her hair down and wore make-up, too much make-up. On days when she skipped the hour-long bus ride and got a fifteen-minute ride home with Russell Schmidt to the end of our drive-way, she went over to the Cafe, lathered on the lipstick and hung out with Shirley Clapstein and the gang. For Likely, that was crazy.

Likely School was a six-room affair with students in grades 1 to 12 all jumbled together. I saw Louise's exploits first-hand. In fact I got wise and threatened to tell Mom and Dad about Louise and her make-up, and about Russell Schmidt, if she didn't let me hang out at the Cafe and some-times get a ride home in Russell's '52 Fargo. I sat alone at a separate table with my bribe Fanta and French fries and tried to look cool.

Russell was cool. He was dark and greasy-haired and apathetic and smoked Players and said "Hey," as if that was enough. He leaned against counters, he leaned against cars and, when he walked with Louise around school, he leaned on her. Not that he went to school. That was one of Mom and Dad's biggest objections about him.

"He just hangs around," said my mother. "He does noth-ing but hang around."

"He works," said Louise.

"He's a gas jockey," said my father.

"He's an older boy," said my mother. "Older boys have … appetites."

"Mom!" said Louise. She was a lot more of a prude than she let on at the Cafe. There I heard her talking about a new pill that stopped ladies from having babies; I even heard her say "rubbers," though at the time I thought she was talking galoshes. I got to watching Louise pretty close.

The week of the Miss Hereford contest I saw something on Louise's neck. We were walking up the driveway to the house after Russell had dropped us off at the end of the road, near the mailbox. Louise was wearing one of those sheer, nickel-apiece scarves around her neck. The scarf didn't quite cover a mark about the size and colour of a strawberry.

"You stuck the milker on your neck too?" I said.

Louise touched the spot, then tightened her scarf. She messed my hair and grinned at me. "You bet, gomer," she said.

It felt kind of good, having Louise follow my lead like that.

That evening my mother discovered the mark. She had Louise standing on the table in the green striped strapless evening gown, with straps, that Louise would wear the night of the Miss Hereford contest. My mother had made the dress herself, picked out the material herself, added the straps herself, and was now pinning up the hem to just above the ankles. The cut of the dress held Louise's legs together, so to get up on the table she had to hop onto the kitchen chair and then hop onto the table, a tricky business. Despite the cut of the neckline, Louise still wore the scarf. My mother talked through a mouthful of pins. "Take that thing off," she said.

"I like the scarf," said Louise.

"It doesn't suit the dress. I want to see the effect of the dress with your hair."

"I'm cold," said Louise.

"That scarf doesn't do a thing about the cold," said my mother.

"Can't we just get the hem done? I've got homework."

"Off with it!" said my mother, and she got that pursed-lipped misery look that meant she meant business. Louise slowly pulled the scarf from around her neck, and there it was, plain as day.

"What is that?" said my mother.

"What?" said Louise.

"That's an inflation hickey," I said. "Like mine, remember?"

"Oh, that," said Louise. She grinned and shrugged and tried to look nonchalant.

My mother pursed her lips even further, remembered the pins and spit them into her hand. She made little gasping noises for a moment and then left the room. I looked up at Louise, but she only crossed her arms and stood up there, on our kitchen table. There were low whispers in the bedroom, and my father said, "What!" Then more whispering. After an eternity my father strode out from the bedroom followed by my mother.

"Let's see!" he said. "Get down off that table."

"I can't," said Louise. "I'm pinned."

"Oh, for heaven's sake," said my father. He stood up on a kitchen chair and examined my sister's neck. "You expect us to believe you got that from a milking inflation?"

"You believed Martin."

"Martin's eleven years old! And his hickey is in the middle of his forehead!"

"Then believe what you want."

"You've gone too far, missy," said my mother. "If you want to be treated like a young lady, you've got to act like one. You won't be seeing Russell any more, do you understand me?"

"Yeah, right," said Louise.

My mother pulled Louise down off the table by the elbow. Pins scattered and Louise shrieked as the pins on her hem poked her in the ankles.

"You get this straight," said my mother. "This is no game. That kind of behaviour only leads to trouble. What's going to happen if this young man gets you pregnant? Do you think he's going to be around to support you? What kind of reputation do you think you'll have? You won't finish school."

"Pregnant?" said Louise. "Who said anything about getting pregnant?"

"Haven't you had that talk yet?" said my father.

"I hadn't got around to it," said my mother.

"I think it's past due," said my father.

"I don't need the talk," said Louise. "I know about rubbers and all that."

My mother's face blanched. "Martin, outside!" she said. "Now!"

I shrugged and went to the hallway to put on my socks and boots, coat and hat. I even sought out my winter mittens that were somewhere in a box in the back of the closet. I wanted to get in on as much of this as I could. I had a niggling feeling that Louise might not have gotten the hickey from the inflation cup, and that there might be other ways to get hickeys that were more dangerous and infinitely more fun.

"We've got to make you understand," said my mother. "There's only one way to make you understand. We've been far too lenient with you. Spare the rod and spoil the child!"

"Oh, come on," said Louise. "I'm almost seventeen. I'm not a kid any more."

"Obviously you're not old enough to take responsibility for the freedom we allow you!" said my mother. "You've broken our trust. If you're not going to act responsibly, you'll get a child's punishment."

"Bend over!" said my father. "On my knee!"

"That's indecent!" said Louise.

The hallway was right off the kitchen and I saw it all. My father took Louise by the arm and shoulders and swung her, pins and all, over his knee, and administered one good slap to the green dress that covered her bottom. He immediately stood her upright again. My father looked flushed and embarrassed, and my sister Louise ran off in tight little steps and slammed her bedroom door. My mother stood there with her hands on her hips and sniffed. "Well," she said. "It had to be done."

"She's right, though," said my father. "She's too old for that. She's not a child any more."

"What else do we do?" said my mother.

"Talk to her?" said my father.

"Talk to her! She's got a hickey on her neck. You know how she got a hickey on her neck!"

"I think I remember," said my father. My mother got suddenly angry and marched into their bedroom and slammed that door. My father looked at me, still tying my boots in the hallway, and shrugged. Show over.

Anyway, I had my own problems. I hated showing cattle, and that was what you had to do in the 4-H club. As a consequence I'd left off teaching Elvis, my heifer calf, to lead, that is, to tag along like a dog on a halter. The usual way to get a calf used to a halter is to tie her up for short periods of time when she's still quite young. There are alternatives, if you're in a hurry. Tim Schmidt tied his calf to another calf for about a week, until they both got used to being pulled around. Norman tied his calf to his grandfather's donkey, and that broke her to a halter in less than a day. I hadn't done any of these things, and I didn't have easy access to a donkey.

The day before the fair, Dad got wind that I hadn't taught Elvis to lead and told me if I embarrassed the Winkle good name in that show ring, well he'd, well, he wasn't sure what he'd do, but it wouldn't be good. So there I was, the day of the Miss Hereford competition, pulling on my calf's halter for everything I was worth, in the mud of the barnyard, in the rain. Elvis stood with her legs splayed, head up, stubborn. A calf ready to show weighs 1100 pounds. If she didn't want to go, she wouldn't. She didn't.

When my father had a really mean bull he had to move, he hooked the bull up, on a short halter, to the back of the tractor with the manure-scraper on it, and then slowly pulled the bull to the new pasture. The manure-scraper acted as a barrier between my father and the bull. The most stubborn and dangerous bull would just trot behind the tractor because he could do nothing else. The day of the Miss Hereford contest, I hooked Elvis's halter up to the manure-scraper.

This was not one of my more inspired ideas. Elvis did not trot behind the tractor as my father's bulls did. As I drove slowly around the muddy barnyard, the calf's front feet stumbled, but her back feet remained firmly planted, and she slid like that behind me, leaving two long drag marks.

When I stopped the tractor I found that, in the process of pulling, the halter had rubbed off the hair behind her ears and left blisters there. In an odd way my idea had been successful, because Elvis was so sore behind the ears that, when I pulled the halter, she followed me anywhere. But then she had no hair at the base of her ears; a judge would count that against me. It was a pity because Elvis really was a good calf; she had an excellent chance of winning a trophy, at least that year. Cattle breeding goes through as many trends as the fashion industry. The year of the first Miss Hereford contest, a Hereford could not have a sway back or a round rump. She had to be purebred. She had to be square. That year a "good calf" meant an animal that looked like a cardboard box on legs, as Elvis did. The same seemed to go for the contestants of the Miss Hereford contest. The Miss Hereford contest at the best of times wasn't exactly a beauty contest. The beauties of any given town weren't likely the daughters of farmers. They were the daughters of teachers, lawyers and plumbers whose families had the bucks to keep their daughters' clothes new and their homes equipped with plumbing.

The night of the Miss Hereford contest my sister wore that strapped strapless gown and a green carnation in her hair (Mom insisted), and the scarf around her neck. She sat on a chair on top of the baptismal tank, which was covered with a piece of plywood that acted as the stage. From where I was sitting all I could see above Pastor Gottlieb's pulpit was the green carnation. There were five other contestants arranged on the half-circle of chairs. Noreen Doose was wearing a pink cloud; Carol Wyton was in a sugary affair that sparkled under the pulpit light; Bev Deacon graced the stage in a navy dress her mother might have worn when she greeted her husband on his return from the war; and June Dyck wore a carrot-coloured shift to match her hair. Then there was Gudrun Hammerstein.

"She's bully," my dad had said about Gudrun earlier, when we were feeding the calves, when my mother wasn't around. Bully cows look too much like bulls and never catch — that is, they don't get pregnant. Tonight Gudrun was the only one looking calm. While all the other contestants fiddled with their wrist corsages, she chewed gum and surveyed the filling pews. Pastor Gottlieb was the master of ceremonies for the event. He sat beside the pulpit, scandalously holding the hand of his young wife, Samantha. His toupee was a little off the mark, and the lights above caught a bald spot and reflected stunningly; it held my attention for much of the night.

The two judges had been voted in by the Hereford Breeders' Club before the contestants were chosen, so that nobody would complain. Mrs. Noyes, a widow and my teacher, was nominated for her "expertise on social graces" by Rudy Bierlie, who was sweet on her, and voted in because everyone was too polite to say otherwise. Gordon Bragg, editor of the county newspaper, the *Leduc Representative*, was nominated without his knowledge by Mr. Hammerstein and voted in because everybody thought it was a good idea. Maybe Gordon Bragg was flattered; in any case he turned up to do the judging, and brought his camera.

I sat between my mother and father in our pew in church, half thinking about the episode of *My Favorite Martian* I'd seen the night before, half listening to Evangeline Hammerstein chatting up a storm with Mrs. Mulder in the pew behind us. Evangeline Hammerstein was Wallace Hammerstein's wife, mother of bully Gudrun. On the occasions when Mrs. Hammerstein taught Sunday school she made me feel as if there wasn't much point in trying to grow up. "We're all sinners," she told us. "Judgement day is upon us. The Lord will find each of us sinning and we'll be judged for those sins." Her message was plain: the world was coming to an end, and we'd all be caught with our hands in the Cookie Jar of Life when the Great Baker came to find us. She gave you the feeling she was the only one on earth who didn't like cookies.

"Look at that," said Mrs. Hammerstein. "Did you see that?"

"Well, kids is kids," said Mrs. Mulder.

"No child of mine would ever look like that," said Mrs. Hammerstein.

It occurred to me that maybe I was the object of their attention. I did a quick survey of my Sunday clothes to see if anything was sticking up or sticking out. Evidently my mother was thinking the same thing. She took out her comb and flattened my hair.

"That's terrible," said Mrs. Hammerstein. "Imagine."

I batted my mother's hand away and tried to turn around to see what Mrs. Hammerstein and Mrs. Mulder were looking at. All I could see was Nevil making faces at Norman. Nothing out of the ordinary there. "That Shute boy is always at it," said Mrs. Mulder.

"It's his mother who's to blame," said Mrs. Hammerstein. "If she had more control over him … "

My mother had said the same thing about Nevil and his mother on occasion. But she didn't like Mrs. Hammerstein, and she was a bundle of nerves this evening, what with Louise in the contest and all. She turned in the pew and hissed the biblical paraphrase, "Why do you look at the speck in your brother's eye, but don't notice the log in your own?" That shut Evangeline up because her own son, Wally, stole jars of pickles from the General Store at lunch hour, ate them all at once and then drank the vinegary juice until his lips turned white. His favourite game was running over cats' tails with his bicycle, for the sound the cats made, although he did that less now. The cats in town had gotten wise.

My father crossed his legs and arms and settled his face into one hand. Nevil pulled a face at me, so I pulled at the sides of my mouth and rolled my eyes. Mom slapped me across the hands, and I felt the sting through what there was of the Miss Hereford pageant.

Gudrun was the first to get up and give the requisite speech on Herefords. She was still chewing gum and she shifted back and forth on her high heels behind the pulpit, precisely like a cow bothered by flies. "Herefords fatten fast and their fat marbles well," she read. "When you cut into a Hereford steak, the flecks of fat is what makes it juicy. A Hereford will gain weight on grass, that's a fact."

Of course it was then the impossible happened. Gudrun Hammerstein stepped back, and the heel of her shoe stuck in the space between the plywood lid on the baptismal tank and the tank itself. She went down, and with enough force to dislodge the tank lid and the other contestants. Noreen Doose fell backward into the tank with Gudrun, and my sister fell forward into the front pew over Miss Short Horn, Miss Heavy Horse and the Pork Princess who'd come all the way from Wetaskiwin to represent their clubs at this event. Russell Schmidt ran from the back of the church, where he'd been keeping out of my mother's sight, up to the front faster than Mom could untangle herself from the people in her pew. He wrapped an arm around Louise and sprang her out the side door.

Gudrun, of course, was Miss Hereford 1969. Pastor Gottlieb conferred with the judges and announced that since the Likely Fair was the next day, a Miss Hereford had to be decided on that night, and the judges had decided on Gudrun. She had, after all, sold the most raffle tickets; her father had bought three hundred. We didn't hear about all that until later, because Mom was out that side door as fast as she could drag me, hollering, against the flow of the crowd. Of course we weren't fast enough. Louise and Russell were already a flash of dust heading towards Joe

Lake. Dad finally worked his way though the crowd and stood behind Mom holding her shoulders. "You shouldn't have pushed her, Elsie," he said. "She didn't want this. She's not a child any more."

"So how come it's okay to push kids around?" I said. I guess it was the wrong thing to say. Mom had me by the collar and I was in the back of the pickup and we were home before I had a chance to get cold.

The next day, the day of the Likely Fair, I was too concerned with my own worries to care much about the rift between my mother and Louise, although there was so much tension at breakfast that the kitchen would've exploded if I'd let one rip. I kept my gas to myself until after breakfast when I went outside to the barn. Bjarne Lindskoog had come over with his shears to help my dad and me groom my Hereford calf, Elvis.

Bjarne Lindskoog was famous in Likely for the length and noise of his farts. "Yah, so I can out fart anybody," he said, and gave it a try.

I said, "Oh, yeah?" and let a good one go, I thought. But my Dad's was longer, louder and more vile.

"So," said Bjarne Lindskoog, "can you spit into that bucket?" The bucket was halfway across to the milking parlour.

"Sure," I said. I spit clear across it and splatted a good gob on the parlour door.

"Yah, he's got talent," said Bjarne Lindskoog.

The fashion was, then, to shave the show calf from neck to nose, a kind of buzz cut, like mine. She didn't need any trimming around the ears, of course.

"How'd she get such sore ears?" said Lindskoog.

"I don't know," I said and plastered what I thought was an innocent expression on my face. Lindskoog looked sideways at me but let it go. We gave Elvis her haircut, put a halter with extra-wide straps on her to hide the missing hair behind her ears, loaded her up and took her to the barns on the fairgrounds. We then went downtown for the parade.

Everyone turned out for the Fall Fair parade. It was an excuse to take the day off from field work in this "easy season" when every farmer in the region was working eighteen-hour days to get the crop out before rain, frost, freak snowstorms, hail or wind turned the fields into a tractor-sucking mess or flattened the crops to nothing. Anyone who did not attend was branded a self-righteous so-and-so because their industriousness made everyone else look bad. So strong was this notion that two years earlier Golda Lindskoog, bedridden with a fever of 102°, had dragged herself out of bed and stood in the crowd, swaying, until she fainted and had to be loaded up on the 4-H hay wagon and trucked off to Camrose hospital.

Likely had, and still has, the peculiar feature of a horseshoe-shaped main street, Centre Avenue, that ends almost where it begins. Centre Avenue starts on Centre Street and ends on Centre Street two blocks down. There are only two other streets to worry about, First Street and Second Street.

The parade followed Centre Avenue, starting at the new school, one of those flat box buildings with roofs that had to be shovelled off every time there was a good snowfall. The old schoolhouse directly behind the new one was, this day, the fair building; the field, barn and outbuildings behind it were the fairgrounds. When I say fairgrounds, I don't mean to say we had a midway or anything like it. A fair in Likely was a good old-fashioned event with pie and preserve competitions, prizes for the best quilts and afghans, ribbons for truly excellent beasts and showmanship, and lots of ice cream and popcorn.

Up from the new school was a patch of mud and bush where the older kids went to smoke. Here Centre Avenue started to curve north and the town began in earnest. There was the Hotel, which housed the Tavern and the Cafe. Next to that was the General Store. The store had an oiled wood floor, vegetable coolers along the north wall and odd greenish paint on all the walls. The shelves were arranged in rows too close together. No more than three people could shop there comfortably at a time, and buggies wouldn't fit through the isles, so my mother would get an armful, take it to the counter, and go back for another armful until she'd gathered her grocery order. Then she'd pay. The front counter was always crowded with other people's groceries, and my mother would invariably come home with something completely out of character for our household that had got into the grocery bag by mistake, like a box of Betty Crocker cake mix or Chinese noodles.

Once past the store, Centre Avenue might as well have been called Hammerstein Avenue, because the Hammerstein family had things pretty much sewed up there. Wallace Hammerstein's tractor dealership and hardware store stood at the point where the street started back on itself, and next to him was his younger brother Ed's garage and butcher shop.

The parade began with two bored rookie R.C.M.P. officers in a police car who must have been borrowed from Leduc. They were followed by the school's baton-twirling squad of three girls who dropped their sticks all the way down the street. Next came several little kids dressed as clowns and riding tricycles, followed by the Likely ambulance, driven by Rudy Bierlie in his John Deere cap. Wallace Hammerstein sat dangerously on the top of the cab, throwing waxed-paper-covered balls of fudge at the crowd. The

Likely ambulance was a pickup truck with a purple wood box frame on the back. It owed its existence to Golda Lindskoog's fainting incident, which had thrown a shock of concern through the community. Wallace Hammerstein had been asked to contribute the paint for the ambulance after Lindskoog contributed his old pickup. The cans of purple paint Hammerstein donated had been sold to him by a salesman who said purple was the colour of the sixties. Hammerstein had bought them on the hunch that the man was right, never figuring the sixties wouldn't happen in Likely.

After the purple ambulance came the 4-H float. 4-H had fallen on hard times in Likely. A provincial club needs a quorum of eight members in Alberta, and there just weren't many kids interested in farming any more. So several clubs teamed up to get enough members together. This year the float was offered up by the Pork, Beef, Debating and Photography 4-H club of Likely. As always, the 4-H float was a hay wagon driven by Bjarne Lindskoog. There wasn't so much as a camera or pig on it, only us kids and a tattered sheet of newsprint roll-end with "4-H" scrawled across it in black felt pen.

Behind the 4-H float Wallace's father, Able Hammerstein, went by on his brand-new Minneapolis Moline propane tractor. He wasn't actually part of the parade; he was just driving from his south pasture to his north, and Centre Avenue was the most convenient path. Able didn't take much stock in celebrations of any kind, and this was his way of showing everybody they'd all be better off if they quit messing around with this fun business and got their crops harvested before winter settled in. He was the one exception to the ethic that kept us all coming out for the parade, but as he didn't go to church on Sunday and work

was the only comfort he had, he was forgiven for this tres-
pass. Nevertheless he cast a sour note on the parade and, as
folks started drifting back to their cars after he went by, he
pretty much ended it.

Me and Nevil and the other 4-H kids headed back to the
livestock barns and spent the rest of the morning greasing up
our calves, brushing our horses and washing down our
swine. Miss Hereford made the rounds of the fairground
like a proud chicken, talking to 4-H leaders and awarding
ribbons. She was dressed in tight jeans, a plaid shirt, a cowboy hat, cowboy boots, a ribbon that said "Miss Hereford
1969" and lipstick.

"She don't look so bad," said my father.

"She's bully," said my mother.

My sister wasn't saying anything. She sat on a bale of hay,
petting the cat that lived in the livestock barns. She hadn't
said anything since breakfast, and what she'd said then was,
"Do I have to ask permission to breathe?" I was jumpy like
a Mexican bean. I'd had two sticks of cotton candy, a bar of
toffee and three bottles of Fanta, and the 4-H Hereford
show was in one half hour. Mom was standing there in her
sensible brown shoes and Dad hadn't laughed when I told
him how Russell's younger brother Tim Schmidt had been
brushing down his dairy calf's back legs when the calf got
himself a case of the shits. Then my mother says, "What
kind of contest was that, anyway? Where the winner is
decided beforehand?"

"Stupid contest," says Louise. "Like I said, and you
wouldn't listen."

"I think I'll go over and talk to Lindskoog for a while,"
says Dad, and he's off like a shot towards the show ring. I'm
stuck there holding the rope to my calf.

"You would have won," says my mother.

"I don't care about winning," says Louise.

My mother looks at me like she wants to tell me to go do chores, but she just sits on the bale of hay with her back to Louise. They sit like that for a while, back to back.

Then Mom says, "There was a young man I had a crush on when I was in school."

Louise says, "I heard that story."

"No," says my mother. "Not your father. There was a young man I met that year at college." Louise looks surprised, maybe a little scared, like she doesn't want to hear this, but she's got her back to Mom, so Mom doesn't see. "He wasn't very tall, or even good-looking," says Mom. "But there was something about him ... anyway, he smoked. He played cards. And, as it turned out, he could never keep a job. He was from a bad family."

"Give me a break," says Louise.

"Hear me out," says my mother, and they're both quiet. After a minute, Mom says, "I didn't see all that. All I saw was the hair on his arms and the way he made me feel. He made me feel ... like nothing much else mattered."

"So the point of the story is I should stop dating such a jerk, right?"

"The point is ... the point is your grandmother and grandfather told him to stop seeing me, and he did."

"Jerk," says Louise.

"It doesn't matter. It was for the best. But I hated my mother for that. I don't think I've ever forgiven her. And here I am."

My mother and my sister are quiet for a while, then Louise says, "Russell's got the hairiest arms." They both laugh for a bit, and then they're quiet, looking off into space as if me and this barn aren't even there. I'm standing there holding the tether to my calf and kicking sawdust and feel-

ing sick from them fighting, or maybe it's gas, and then —
just like that — it's 2:20 in the afternoon and Bjarne
Lindskoog's voice is over the crackly PA system saying,
"Yah, so you in junior Hereford bring your calves to the
ring," and I'm walking like a sleepwalker, leading my
Hereford calf to the show ring where maybe I'll lose, but
maybe I'll win.

A GOLDEN HEMORRHOID

T HE city kid, Alex Cooperman, was quick to figure
out the schoolground hierarchy. At noon and recess
— when we threw a football around the field —
Alex ran up to the guys, his face red and eyes looking crazy,
and grabbed their balls hard and yelled, "Gotcha." He never
did that to me; maybe he thought he didn't have to.

He dared us to go to the Ditch — the marshy boundary
between the playing field and the bush, the forbidden zone.
Older kids went into the bush to smoke and worse, although
I wasn't sure what worse was. "You never go over there?"
Alex said.

"Older kids go there," said Peggy. "The ones that get in
trouble."

"That Slabie kid goes there, every day," said Alex. "She
don't get in trouble."

"She doesn't go into the bush," said Judy.

"Slabie's a porker," said Norman. That's what we yelled
at Dorothy: Slabie's a porker. Or, Slab of Pork. Or, Bacon.
Not me. I never called her names, on principle, but then I
was never nice to her either. She sat on a stump at the Ditch
every noon and recess, and after school before the bus came,
eating something brown and rolled and foreign: she never

brought sandwiches. The rumour was her underwear was made from cotton sugar sacks, just like in the Depression. Judy and Peggy said you could still see "Sugar" written across the backside of Dorothy's underwear, if you could get a look.

"If Slabie can go there, anybody can go there," said Alex. He assembled us near the bush, a little way from where Dorothy Slabie sat on her stump. We looked around for a dry spot to sit, but there wasn't one, and none of us would go back to school to eat lunch, not with Alex standing there. Instead we stood in the marshy grass and unrolled our lunch bags (Alex said lunch boxes were stupid), and peeled our oranges with our Tupperware orange peelers (no one brought one to school until Alex brought his), and ate our Velveeta, ham and pickle sandwiches (Alex's favourite). I watched the water squoosh to the surface of the grass as I put my weight on one foot and then the other. Peggy and Judy traded half-sandwiches (Peggy's mom used white bread, Judy's used brown). Alex was saying how he'd bet nobody there even knew what sex was. He said it to sound like a snake, to taunt us. "SSSex," he said.

"Man's on top," said Norman. "I saw pictures at Joe Lake." Joe Lake General Store was known for its row of *those* magazines, kept above the cigarettes, far above the hands of anyone at Likely School.

"You're lying," said Judy.

"Am not," said Norman.

My best friend, Nevil Shute, spoke in Norman's defence. "Bull gets on top. They get on behind."

"Just like the pictures," said Norman. "She had big tits like this. Put a milking machine on her, eh?" Norman never used words like "tits" before Alex turned up, and Peggy and Judy didn't like it one bit.

"You're gross," said Peggy and grabbed Judy's hand, and

they ran towards the swings. We all stood around kicking grass for a while.

"She's just jealous 'cause she doesn't have tits," said Norman.

"It's the swearing; it's not nice to swear," I said, and I meant it. Pastor Gottlieb said uttering profanities was a sin, and I believed it. Pastor Gottlieb said dinosaurs were a myth, and I believed that too.

"What a fag," said Alex. "Bet you never swore before in your life."

"Martin's swore before, plenty of times," said Nevil. Nevil and I once got a ride in the back of my dad's pickup and said "hell" every time we saw a crow. We giggled until my gut ached.

"He's never swore," said Alex. "Say goddamn, Martin, say Christ, like you mean it."

Pastor Gottlieb's face flashed into my head, and my father's, and, worse yet, my mother's. I know my face went red. Alex told me so. "See, he can't say it," he said. "Say god-damn, Martin, say Jesus Harry Christ."

"Don't be dumb," said Nevil. "Martin swears. He just doesn't swear in front of girls. It isn't polite."

"Martin likes Judy," said Norman and poked me in the belly. "Martin's got a girlfriend."

"Shut up," I said. "Do not."

"Naw, he's never even kissed a girl," said Alex. At Bible camp our cabin counsellor, Ted, had a girlfriend who was the cook's helper, and Ted warned us he'd get her to come and kiss us goodnight if we didn't get quiet. I was mortified. Ted's girlfriend smoked; I'd seen her back of the cookhouse when she thought no one was looking. Seeing her smoke gave me a hard-on. If she kissed me I'd go to hell. Or worse, Mom would find out. The thought of Ted's girlfriend kissing me turned me inside out and upside down and I ended up in the sleeping bag head first so all she'd get were my feet. It was weird waking up with my head encased like that.

"Leave him alone," said Nevil. "You're the one with the girlfriends. Norman the worm makes all the girls squirm."

"You're just jealous," said Norman. "Hey, Dorothy, Alex thinks you're pretty." Dorothy Slabie looked across the field and ruminated her lunch. She ignored us with the grace of a sloth. "What a cow," said Norman.

"Dorothy likes you," said Alex. "Hey, Porker ... Dorothy, Norman wants to fuck you." The word "fuck" still wielded a terrible and powerful wallop then, and its invocation shocked us into silence and ran a visible chill through Dorothy Slabie. She rolled a piece of waxed paper into a ball, placed it in her plastic lunch box, wiped the crumbs off her skirt and, very slowly, walked down the sidelines of the field to the school. I went back to watching the water squoosh between my feet. The word "fuck" was vibrating hot in my cheeks. I didn't say anything to Alex. For that, and a lot of other things, I'm sorry, Dorothy. "Dumb bitch," said Alex.

"I'm getting a drink of water," said Norman, and we watched him cross the field and meet up with Judy and Peggy at the swings.

"He's a dork," said Alex. He kicked the grass, and after a while he looked at me, and at Nevil. "You ever?" said Alex.

"What?" said Nevil.

"You know. Like when you wake up and your bed's wet."

"Jeez," said Nevil and looked around. "I don't wet the bed."

"No, not that," said Alex. "Like when you have a dream or something. But when you do it to yourself. You know, jerking off." He made a gesture like he was shaking up a pop bottle.

"You are gross," said Nevil.

It was while I was doing the chores that evening that it occurred to me what Alex and Nevil had been talking about. That meant somebody else did it too. I knew it was bad, or at least I couldn't talk about it, but somehow I felt better knowing somebody else did it. I thought maybe even Nevil did it, the way he looked embarrassed. That evening I was caring for a calf with a prolapsed rectum. It happens. Bull calves jump up and ride cows as soon as their front legs reach a cow's pin bones. My father said he'd never seen a bull calf jump as much as this one. "He'll be a breeder," he told me. "Hang on to him, Martin." The down side is that these calves get to jumping so much their rectums prolapse; that is, their rectums get swollen and hang outside, and the calves are open to infection. If they aren't treated, and aren't forced to take a break from all that jumping, they'll die trying.

In the middle of filling this calf's water bucket, I realized there was some connection between what Alex called jerking off, and the way the bull calves jumped the cows, and the way babies turned up. Even Nevil had said that; he'd said the bulls get on top. I knew when a bull got on top of a cow, the cow had a calf. But I didn't get on top of anybody, although once I put a pillow between my legs.

Then I had a thought: if I did that too much, would my rectum prolapse?

I hurried to finish chores; the sick calf took forever. His pen needed extra careful cleaning because the vet was coming in the morning. My gut had tightened so much by supper that I couldn't eat. My mother felt my forehead, examined the paleness under my eyes and declared me sick. She made me stay home from school the next day. Lying in bed, I had too much time to mull over my terror. I thought of my Uncle George, who complained about his hemorrhoids when he came over for dinner, how he couldn't sit down without feeling pain. Once when I asked what they were, my mother said hemorrhoids came from pushing too hard when you're constipated. But what if she was wrong, or being polite? Uncle George never showed Aunt Gilda anything like affection; what if you got hemorrhoids from jerking off?

I tried reading. I picked up my social studies text, but on the cover was a collage of photographs, including one of a half-naked African woman. I threw down the textbook and looked at the Bible that sat on the night table next to my bed. I couldn't pick it up. I stared at the letters on the cover and they clouded over. I found myself thinking about what Alex had said, about my bull calf, about jerking off. As if guided by the hand of God, my mother turned on the radio in the kitchen. Dr. Goldheim, the Converted Jew, was reading from First Samuel. " 'Now the hand of the Lord was heavy on the Ashdodites,' " he said, " 'and He ravaged them and smote them with hemorrhoids.' They'd stolen the ark of the Covenant and God sent on them a plague of mice and hemorrhoids. What could they do to stop the wrath of God? Let me read further. They said, 'What shall be the guilt offering which we shall return to Him?' and the priests and diviners said, 'Five golden hemorrhoids and five golden mice.' "

I knew I'd been spoken to. I'd been smitten for my wrongdoing, but I could get off the hook by coming up with a guilt offering worthy of my sin. I couldn't afford a golden rectum; I couldn't imagine where I'd get one if I could. But I could sell my bull calf and send the money to Dr. Goldheim. I silently confessed my sin of jerking off and swore never to do it again. I dressed, convinced my mother I was okay by letting her feel my forehead, and went outside. I'd talk to my father about my plan, at least about selling the calf. Oscar Podritski, the vet, was out in the barnyard with my father; they had my bull calf in the chute. My father had the calf's tail up in the air, and Oscar was sewing up its rear end. He went in and out of the skin around the calf's rectum with a huge needle, and when he was finished he pulled the string up tight, as if the calf's behind were a gunny sack. "Worst prolapse I've seen," said Oscar. "He was damn near shitting out his balls."

"Horniest calf I've ever seen," said my father. Then he noticed me. "What're you doing out here? Get back inside if you're so sick."

I went back in the house and locked myself into the bathroom. I couldn't sell the calf, not now, not until it got better. Who would buy it? Worse, I suspected that not only would my rectum fall out, but my balls would fall off, and my penis too. I was doomed by a thing I didn't understand. I pulled down my pants, sat on the toilet and tried to get a look; everything seemed the same. It didn't look like I was losing anything. Not yet.

The next day I couldn't eat the lunch Mom sent, my stomach was so tied in knots. I only picked at supper. The day after that Mom declared me pale and made me eat oatmeal and cream for breakfast. At school I felt constipated, but there was no way I was going to go to the bathroom to push. I squirmed in my chair; I couldn't concentrate on anything but the discomfort of my behind against the hard seat of my desk. Mrs. Noyes droned on about some place in Africa where nobody had ever seen snow.

I had to fart. I had to. It was a loud fart, the loudest ever. It caught the wood in the schoolroom and resonated, and the whole class got the giggles, and that resonated too. I knew if I blushed — if I didn't laugh — everybody would know it was me. So I laughed too, and played it cool, and would have been safe, if it weren't for Mrs. Noyes.

Mrs. Noyes wore two wigs, blonde and brunette. When she was blonde she wore high heels; when she was brunette she wore spectacles and sensible shoes. When she was blonde, she was perky and pleasant and told stories about her mother making pudding on a wood stove. When she was brunette, she wore brown clothes and carried a yardstick and told us about her father, a sergeant in the First World War, who'd been buried alive and then unburied by two separate grenades that left little bits of shrapnel in his head. Today she was brunette. "Shut up," she said. "Shut up!"

Everybody shut up. Mrs. Noyes slapped the yardstick against the palm of her hand and walked between the rows, sniffing. "Who was it?" she said. "Answer me!" Nobody said anything, but everybody looked around. Dorothy was the only one not looking around.

"It was Dorothy," said Alex. He was on the other side of the room, up front, so Mrs. Noyes could keep an eye on him. "Stinky Dorothy. She's only got one pair of underwear."

"Be quiet!" said Mrs. Noyes. "Dorothy wouldn't think of making a noise like that. That was a boy noise."

That was how I came to believe that girls did not fart.

Mrs. Noyes slapped the yardstick and went down the rows asking each boy, "Did you make a smelly noise, Steven?" "Did you, Norman?"

"Did you, Martin?" The whole class turned in their desks and looked at me. I couldn't say anything. My chest hurt. The classroom rolled and bucked. I thought I'd faint. The class snickered. "Quiet!" said Mrs. Noyes. "Turn around!" The class faced the front, rigid. "We do not make smelly noises in public, Martin," said Mrs. Noyes. "Smelly noises are only made in the bathroom. Hold out your hands."

"I couldn't help it," I said, but I was too late. She'd

already brought the yardstick, edge to skin like a knife, down across my hands. It hurt, it hurt like hell, but more than that I was hearing the voice of my big sister, Louise, saying how you can always tell a kid who gets in trouble by the permanent red marks on his hands. I was marked for life. Mrs. Noyes adjusted her glasses and marched to the front of the class to tell us about the Masai warriors who wore bits of Goodyear tires for sandals on the streets of Nairobi. I bit my lip and tried not to cry because Mrs. Noyes the brunette didn't like that either. Boys didn't cry.

Beside me, Dorothy Slabie very deliberately put down her pencil, tapped her desk lightly twice, and made the sign for "Okay." She did all this looking straight ahead, at Mrs. Noyes, and nobody else could have seen it. She meant it for me. She was telling me it was okay, no big deal, me farting. She was bestowing on me a kindness.

On Sunday Pastor Gottlieb was all riled up. He was fresh back from a week spent volunteering at the street mission in Edmonton, where he'd evangelized to male prostitutes posing on the streets, and women in slacks passing by to do their shopping, and waiters dressed as the Queen at Her Majesty's Dinner Theatre (until the management asked him to leave). His theme for the service was "Unlawful Sexual Relations and Cross-dressing," and his reasons for giving this sermon were clear enough. There weren't any men dressing up in skirts in Likely, not that anyone knew about, but there were plenty of women casting off their skirts and doing their chores, even going into town, dressed in jeans and slacks. Golda Lindskoog even wore pantsuits to church. It was practically an epidemic.

"It's right here in the word of God!" said Pastor Gottlieb. "Deuteronomy 22:5. 'A woman shall not wear man's clothing, nor shall a man put on a woman's clothing; for whoever does these things is an abomination to the Lord your God.'"

Then he went on to tell us about the wickedness rampant in the city of Edmonton, and quoted a lot from Leviticus about what God allowed in the way of a good time, and much more about what he didn't allow, and how "if a man lies with a man as one lies with a woman, both of them have done what is detestable" and they must be put to death, and all that. "They act like cattle in that city," said Pastor Gottlieb. "We aren't built like cattle, and we're not meant to act like cattle." We all knew what he was talking about. Each and every day we all went out into our pastures and watched for signs of heat — when a cow is ready to impregnate — and that meant watching for cows mounting other cows. When you were picking a bull, you would look for one that mounted other bulls in the bull pen — a bull so oversexed he couldn't control himself. Gay love was rampant in the bovine world.

I was somewhat comforted by Pastor Gottlieb's sermon. Obviously God, talking through Pastor Gottlieb, was saying that I, Martin, wasn't built like a bull calf. My rectum wouldn't fall out. Even so, I left the service feeling guilty because my mother sometimes made me put on her terry-cloth bathrobe after a bath.

After church my mother and father stayed for coffee and sent me along home as a chaperone for Russell and Louise. Mom and Dad were letting Louise see Russell, because Mom had finally figured out she couldn't do anything to stop it. But, whenever she could, Mom arranged things so Louise and Russell were not alone.

Russell didn't take me and Louise straight home, though. On the way they just looked at each other, and he turned off to Joe Lake. "What about him?" said Louise. I was "him," and him was sitting as close as he could to the passenger door because Russell had his arm around Louise's shoulder and was feeling it up pretty good.

"He'll be okay in the truck," said Russell.

"What are we going this way for?" I said.

Louise shrugged off Russell and gave me her I'll-get-you look. "Don't you tell Mom," she said. "You do and I'll tell her you bought cigarettes for that Alex kid."

I gave her the don't-be-stupid look and nodded. "Where we going?" I said.

"Joe Lake," she said.

"Fishing?" I said. I liked fishing.

Louise and Russell looked at each other. Russell snorted. "Yeah, fishing," he said. I didn't trust Russell. He was always getting friendly, getting my hopes up and then letting me down.

"We don't got poles," I said.

"I got a knife, don't I?" said Russell. "Twine in the back. Louise, got a safety pin?"

"Sure," said Louise.

"You find us a worm," said Russell, "and we're fishing." He grinned at me. I gave him the don't-be-stupid look just in case.

Russell parked the truck near a poplar stand and handed me his jackknife and a piece of binder twine. "Here," he said. "Find a pole and fish down there." He pointed to a rock outcrop about a mile, it seemed, down the lake. "Louise and me'll do our fishing here."

Russell pulled Louise back in the truck. Russell wasn't doing any fishing. All he wanted was to be alone with her. I trudged down the shoreline and didn't look back once. The remarkable thing was, I caught a fish, the biggest trout ever. I ran back to the truck dangling my fish by Louise's safety pin, so excited I dropped the fish twice. When I got back to the truck, nobody was there. "Louise?" I said.

Grasshoppers and a few gophers whistled off somewhere. There was a fresh trail through the grass, running from the truck to the poplar stand. I laid the fish in the grass by the truck and listened. After a few moments I heard Louise cry out, "Quit that!" and giggle. I ran to her voice, through the fresh trail. She and Russell were rustling around in the grass. A tickle fight? Wrestling? Her skirt was all bunched up and Russell, in his underwear, was lying on her, pinning her down; the backs of his legs were hairy. I got all shy and ran back to the truck, feeling panicked, as if I were being chased; I jumped in the back of the pickup and stayed there with my fish until Russell and Louise came out of the bush flushed and blurry-eyed. I held up the fish. "Look what I caught," I said.

"You can't take that home," she said.

"What d'you mean?"

"How are you going to explain it to Mom?"

"I don't care," I said.

"I'll tell about the smokes," she said, and when I didn't answer she said, through her teeth, "I mean it." I was getting stingey eyes. I'd never caught a fish before, at least not one big enough to keep. I wanted with all my heart to show Dad. "Martin," said Louise, and her voice sounded just like Mom's. I threw the fish at her feet. I missed. She handed me the roll of toilet paper Russell kept in his truck. "Clean your hands," she said. "You smell like a fish."

"You stink like a cow," I said.

"Don't be dumb," she said. I stayed in the back of the pickup and ignored them all the way home and didn't even say thanks for the ride when Russell dropped us off at the end of the driveway.

It was while Dad and I were sitting on the tractor looking over the herd for signs of heat that it occurred to me what Louise and Russell had been doing in the poplar grove. That was sex. Norman was wrong; it wasn't anything like what the cattle did. Right then I had to tell Dad about the fish, I had to, so I lied. "When Nevil and me were at camp," I said, "I caught a trout like this." I held out my arms. "Must've been a two-pounder."

"You never told me about that," said Dad.

"Just remembered," I said. I counted that as my first real lie — I didn't count the ones I told to get out of a belting — and I hated Louise for it.

About two weeks after my calf's rectum got sewed up, Alex asked me to help him find his watch. The watch had fallen off as Alex was chasing Randy, playing his "Gotcha" game. He'd felt it fling off, but kept after Randy, grabbed his balls, and then the recess bell rang and everybody but us went inside the school. Now we were walking alone along the side of the empty field, searching through the grass. Alex asking me to help him was an honour, even if it meant a mild scolding from Mrs. Noyes for coming in from recess late. The scolding wouldn't be bad. She was blonde that day. I felt a rush of thankfulness for Alex's attention, and suddenly I wanted to tell him everything, every embarrassment, every need, every wish I had. It was the desire to bare all, to be understood.

"You remember what you said," I said, tentatively, "about having dreams. About doing it to yourself."

Alex stopped searching the grass and looked back at the school. "Ah, I was just joking," he said.

"Can anything happen?" I said.

"What, like you go blind?"

"I can go blind?"

"No, man. It's just a story; as if your cock's got anything to do with your eyeballs. It's just to stop you from doing it. Like your mom says your face'll stay that way if you do this." He pulled an ape face. "Everybody does it," he said. "Don't you know anything?"

I kicked a rock and watched it bounce through the grass. "What a fag," said Alex.

I was disappointed. Alex wasn't my friend, not a real friend. I'd never be able to tell him my plans, not like I could tell Nevil. But at the same time I felt lifted, freer; confession does that.

"Say Christ," said Alex. "Say it."

"Christ," I said.

"No, like you mean it," said Alex. "Say Jesus Harry Christ!"

"Jesus Harry Christ!" I repeated, and felt sick.

"Hey," said Alex. "We got a pool table. You want to come over after school?"

"No," I said. "My mother'll kill me."

"Yeah, well," he said. We kicked the ground. "Noyes is a bitch," said Alex.

"Yeah," I said.

"What a slut," he said. "Don't you just want to fuck her?"

That afternoon, after school, Alex convinced a group of bus kids — the kids who waited around for an hour after school for the bus — to find out for sure if Dorothy Slabie really wore sugar-sack panties. We formed a circle around Dorothy where she sat on her stump. She was eating as if we weren't there. "Dorothy," said Alex. "Show us your under-wear. Or we'll pull it off."

Dorothy sat high enough that she could look over our heads, so Alex stationed himself in front of her and did jumping jacks. Dorothy looked past him, through him, and brought the brown thing she'd been eating up to her mouth. Alex grabbed it out of her hand and threw it on the ground. "Stinky Dorothy, slimy Dorothy," he said. "What's this? Worms? You eat worms? Dorothy eats worms. Dorothy eats worms."

Alex chanted and some of the other kids chanted because he wanted them to. Dorothy closed her lunch box and slid off the stump and started to walk away. Alex jumped ahead of her. Dorothy changed direction. Alex blocked her way. "Don't you like me, Dorothy?" he said. "Show us your underwear, Dorothy."

Dorothy put one arm out and pushed Alex as if she were pushing a heavy door. Alex pushed back hard and she stumbled, gathered herself and stood still. She closed her eyes. "Nobody pushes me," said Alex.

I wish I'd stopped things right there, before Alex pushed Dorothy into the bush. I wish I'd said, "This is stupid," and walked away taking the rest of the kids with me, so he didn't have us there to perform for. But I didn't, and that was what Alex had over us; he knew all it took was a suggestion and there we were, pulling at Dorothy's pleated skirt, yanking at her navy stockings. Dorothy's face didn't show anything at all. Her body, lying there where Alex pushed her down, on burrweed and cleavers, was stiff and ungiving. She kept her eyes shut, not tight, just shut. Her underwear wasn't made from sugar sacks, not that I could see. It was white, and a piece of elastic had come unthreaded and formed a little loop at her waist. I was embarrassed to the point of sickness at seeing her panties, angry at Alex for making us do this, excited over what was happening, terrified of being found out. We all watched as Alex pushed us out of the way, yanked down his jeans and, in his underwear, humped against Dorothy's underwear in a burlesque parody of rape.

The embarrassment of that was too much to bear. The group of us went dead silent and started kicking the ground. Alex must have seen he was losing us, because he got up and zipped his jeans. "Slut," he said to Dorothy. Some of the other kids picked up the new word and said it too before following Alex back to the school.

I stayed a moment longer, watching for breath in Dorothy's stiff body. Her eyes were closed, and she was so still a notion entered my head that Alex might have killed her by bouncing on top of her like that. When she sat up and began arranging her clothes, I turned away quickly and ran towards the school. I didn't know what the word "slut" meant, but I knew from how Alex had said it that it must be an insult, something you'd say of a woman or a girl. I would never hear it again without remembering Dorothy Slabie, with a ring of chanting children around her and Alex pushing and pushing, as she stumbled backwards over the marshy forbidden line into the bush.

TWO O'CLOCK CREEK

E ACH year on my birthday my father took me out to
someplace on the farm and taught me a skill I
would never have guessed I wanted to know.
Among other things, he taught me how to harness a horse
for ploughing and how to make a slingshot from the crotch
of a young willow, an inner tube and an old leather glove.
The morning I turned fourteen my father took me for a
walk along the banks of Two O'Clock Creek, a slow-mov-
ing creek running through our coulee basin. We walked on
either side of the creek, him in his gumboots and me barefoot and carrying my runners. He hadn't told me, yet, what
we were out there for.

My father's red plaid jack-shirt had bits of hay growing
off it like an old ram's coat. He kept a folding knife next to
his watch in his pants pocket, so they clanked together when
he walked. He had on flannel pants, one of two pairs he
wore year-round. In winter he wore long johns underneath.
Under his jack-shirt he wore a white cotton button-up shirt
and silver metal armbands that had belonged to his father,
one on each arm. He watched the crow that was following
us through the poplars. I watched my father scoop up the
long grass and chew and spit it out. While we were walking,

it occurred to me I'd never asked him about the armbands. Nobody else I knew had a father who wore them.

"Why do you wear those armbands?" I said.

"Keeps my shirts from getting in the machinery," he said.

Not such a bad idea, then. Just the year before, Percy Slabie's sleeve had got caught up in the universal joint of the power take-off in his bailer, and Percy was choked to death by his own jacket. At the time my Uncle George had said it was better for a godless man like Percy to go that way than to live through the end times. "Probably better for Percy to die like that than wait for the tribulation," he'd said.

Nearly everyone in Likely talked like that. Pastor Gottlieb had convinced us all that the end times were on us and the signs were everywhere. The Sunday before my fourteenth birthday, Pastor Gottlieb had preached how Russia was rearing up like a crazed bear, lawlessness was rampant and young girls paraded around in revealing clothes. When he said that last part, about the girls in mini-skirts, his voice rose up and spittle flew from his mouth and he left me feeling guilty for sins I hadn't had the chance, yet, to commit. After church, over coffee in my mother's kitchen, Uncle George backed him up on it. "The world can't take it any longer," said Uncle George. "A man can't expect to farm with his sons any more; can't expect his sons to take over. Government telling us to specialize! Enlarge! Run a farm like a business! All the old ways going out the window. The world can't last ten years." Then: "The world can't last five years!"

Aunt Gilda looked out the window, and my mother got up and filled the plate of squares again, but my father nodded in agreement with Uncle George and that left me wondering for my future. I thought it unfair of God to end the world in five years, before I'd had a chance to grow up and get married and have sex.

The worst of it was, much of the world didn't know a thing about the end times. Pastor Gottlieb said it was our duty as Lamentations brethren to go out and tell the wayward about what was coming, which made us feel guilty because all of us were too shy to evangelize. Pastor Gottlieb said those who didn't believe in the end times were only ignorant; they were the ones who needed a good talking to. So I tried. At my accordion lesson that week, I evangelized to Mrs. Shute.

"Do you know about the end times, Mrs. Shute?" I said. "They're coming, you know." My heart was thudding in my ears, I was so nervous. She had to stand close, to place my fingers on the keys, and her breath smelled of the strawberry ice cream we had eaten before the lesson. We'd each eaten a huge bowl of it, and the decadence made me think of Pastor Gottlieb's descriptions of the lustful excesses that preceded the end of the world.

"I know about the end times," said Mrs. Shute. "I've read Revelations. Have you?"

In fact, I hadn't. Pastor Gottlieb's sermons from Revelations frightened me so much I avoided even touching the last pages of the Bible. "There'll be horsemen," I said. "And wars. Sons won't farm with their fathers. Women will wear mini-skirts. Men will wear dresses. Trudeau will come to power. It's all written about and it's happening!"

"The world isn't going to end, Martin," she said. "People have been saying it's going to end for a very long time, and it hasn't. The world changes, it doesn't end. People just don't like change; they get scared."

I turned my face away. I was confused. Pastor Gottlieb was wrong. Mrs. Shute knew about the end times, she wasn't ignorant. But she didn't believe. How could she not believe?

"Well," she said. "You should learn to like change. Travel

a little. Don't stay here all your life. The world only ends for people who stay here."

I thought about what she'd said as my father and I walked along Two O'Clock Creek in deeper grass and brush. Above us, the crow hopped from one side of the creek to the other, from poplar to poplar. My father's side of the creek was easy, grass and Indian paintbrush. My side was wild rose bramble that scratched my legs where my shorts ended. I always went barefoot. My mother said I had horse leather for feet. She said, "You don't have feet. You got hoofs."

"Come on, Dad," I said. "Where are we going?"

"You'll see," he said.

"Are we going to trap something?"

"You'll see," he said.

Many of my father's birthday lessons involved killing an animal. The year before we had gone deer hunting. The day I turned ten he'd given me a .22 and showed me how to pick off a gopher. On my ninth birthday he simply taught me to kill, in an offhand way, so I didn't see it coming. After milking, he'd told me to take the bucket of first milk off the cow who'd just birthed and feed it to the calves. The calf barn was off the milking parlour. It was a dusty little room with only one dirty window to let any light in, but the calves were warm in there, and it wasn't far to carry the bucket. Even so, I spilled the milk struggling to get it into the smaller buckets we used to feed the calves; the cats came yowling as soon as they heard the splash. There were five calves in the one pen, jostling, sucking at my sleeves and pants, bunting at me as they would at their mothers to let down the milk. Feeding calves in an open pen is no party. A week-old calf weighs a hundred pounds and packs a wallop. I bent over to set the buckets down and one calf bunted me hard in the stomach and knocked the wind out of me. It made me mad. I picked up a plastic pipe and started beating the calves around the face to get them to back off. They stepped away for a moment, then came right back after me, pushing and sucking, so I hit them again.

"Be careful with them," said my father. "They're just babies."

I hadn't heard him come in, and the jolt of surprise ran to my toes. I dropped the pipe and put up with the irritation as I fed the rest of the milk to the calves.

That day, the day of my ninth birthday, my father was taking stock, cleaning up, getting rid of odds and ends. "Too many cats around the barn," he said. "Don't have that many mice." Then my father told me the story about the rats. How there were rats all over, brought by the Europeans, and how in the dirty thirties a make-work project had wiped them out. "I'm not about to let them back in the province," he said. He pointed at the spotted cat nursing her kittens near the milk parlour door. "Martin, kill those kittens, will you?" he said, and walked out of the barn. I was left there wondering what the rat story had to do with the cats.

It didn't occur to me to disobey my father, to let the kittens live. The cat, Sweetpea, purred and kneaded the air. I petted her and touched the blind faces of her kittens. I'd never killed anything before. I didn't think to drown them. I found the plastic pipe where I'd left it next to the calf stalls and picked up a kitten. The kitten could've been a ball of wool, it was that light, but I felt the tiny bones through its skin, its quick tic tic heartbeat. I laid the kitten on a board and slammed the pipe down on its head. The mother cat startled and looked at me. The kitten didn't make a sound, but it wasn't dead. Its heartbeat was still there, only faster. One foot pawed out to the air and its mouth opened and shut. I hit it again and again, in panic, until blood came from its nose and mouth, until it was dead. But I couldn't kill the rest. I felt sick and unsure on my feet, as if the ground and the barn were moving away.

The crow cawed and flew over the creek, over to my father's side. My father's jackknife clanked against the watch in his pocket. I said, "What are we looking for?"

"A maple," he said. "A skinny one. Maybe this big." He held up his finger. Big hands. He was a little man, with big scratched hands.

"Then what?" I said.

"Then we cut it. Like a switch."

"You're not teaching me to cut a switch," I said.

"No," said my father.

My father had never used a switch on me, only the belt, and that was bad enough, but once or twice hexd threatened. "If you don't …," he had said, so the words he didn't say licked out and snapped me like the tongue of a switch.

"I only got a switching one time," said my father. "And it wasn't with a stick. I got her with a whip."

A whip is ten feet long and when it bites you it feels like stinging nettle. I thought stinging nettle and felt the spot on my wrist where I got it last. I thought teeth scraping along a blackboard, and I felt that too, though I'd never done it.

"I got a whipping because me and Horace and George were out playing cowboy on the calves and got thrown off," said my father. "So we tried the pigs, and no sooner got thrown off them when my father comes around the corner with a bull whip and Horace and George are over the fence and gone and I'm left there facing my father and that whip."

"He get you?" I said.

"I headed for the chicken house and dove in the space under it and got a taste of the whip on my rear. After a while my father says I could stay there all night for all he cared. When it was getting dark I crawled out and went to bed with nothing to eat, and went to school the next day with nothing."

"What did you do that was so bad?"

"I don't know."

I knew about unfairness. Every week for a while when I was nine or ten, on Saturday morning, the sleep-in morning, my dad took me into town to the General Store. There was a bell on the door and Harry Wyton, the owner, had painted a sign in black letters on the back of a Coke poster: "If we don't have it and can't get it, you don't need it." I always sat on the bench beside the window and drank Fanta and watched Russell Schmidt serve people at the gas pump. Harry said the same thing every week, "Morning at ya, Enfred," and handed Dad a Players. I never saw my father smoke anywhere but there, at the store. Harry blew smoke rings for me and I stuck my fingers in them as they passed. Once Dad said, "Watch this." He sucked the cigarette into his mouth so just the end, burning red, was showing. "Looks like a sow's tit," said Harry.

I said, "Can I try?"

"No, you cannot," said Dad, but he tossed me a quarter, and said, "Get yourself another pop."

At supper that night I said to Louise, "You should see what Dad can do. He takes this cigarette, a lit cigarette, and puts it in his mouth like this." And I sucked back a green bean so just the end was sticking out. I chewed and grinned. "It looks neat," I said.

Dad pushed his mashed potatoes around in his beans. Louise put a hand over her mouth and snickered. Mom sat up real straight like she did when I was in for it, but she didn't say anything. Nobody said anything at all. After supper my father led me outside behind the barn, yanked down my pants and whipped me with my own belt.

My father stopped and the crow landed in the maple tree above him. The maple wasn't much grown, so a lot of its branches were only the size of one of my father's fingers. I crossed the creek and jumped up to the grass on his side and the crow flew off.

"What're you making?" I said.

"You'll see," he said.

My father pulled out his jackknife and cut off a short branch, trimmed it at both ends, slid his knife around the inside of the bark, next to the wood, tapped it and pulled. There was a hollow tube of bark and a core like his finger. He made a couple of notches on the core and a hole to match on the tube of bark, slid the bark back on and gave the whistle a blow. It made a warble like a preacher bird's call, trilling up, spinning down, and from a willow the crow laughed back.

NAVEL GAZING

COWS have their own brand of intuition; they smell a crazy wind before it hits your face. They run and frolic, kick up their heels and run off on their own. A crazy wind comes in gusts, lets up just as you're thinking of pulling up your collar, and catches you off guard like a slap in the face. It's the crazy wind of spring that tells of a storm coming on, like a thrill or a shiver. We were out there — Mom and Dad, Bjarne Lindskoog, Uncle Horace, Nevil Shute and me — helping Yurgen Zerbeen drive his heifers and a few dry cows (pregnant cows that weren't milking) to a pasture a mile down the road. Yurgen Zerbeen and his wife, Ella, were well into their seventies then, when I was sixteen. They ran their dairy farm as they'd run it for forty years, except they needed a little help now and again. They had no children. It's the way in Likely that if you need something done and can't do it yourself, you call up your neighbours. Almost everybody will come over and help, when asked, and almost nobody expects to get paid in cash. You get paid in favours.

So it was that we were helping Yurgen move his heifers and cows, and the crazy wind was on us. Heifers going right and left, heifers kicking and tossing their heads like the

Lutheran girls at the fire-hall dance. "Gonna be a storm," said Yurgen. He was keeping pace with the rest of us behind those cows, even though it was plain he was nursing a knee. Uncle Horace had told me to stick close to Yurgen, to see he didn't fall.

"Could be," I said, "might rain," although the only clouds I saw were over Edmonton way. Mom and Dad, Bjarne and Uncle Horace were fanned out to our right, walking at a fair clip but not hurrying. Nevil Shute was to our left and ahead, running and whooping. "You hunk of crow bait!" he yelled, and took off after a pregnant cow that jumped the fence to the barley field as if she were a heifer.

"He don't know cows," said Yurgen, and pointed at Nevil.

"Didn't grow up farming," I said. "Mother works in a bank."

"He'll learn soon enough, I expect," said Yurgen.

The cow was jumping ditches and fences, zig-zagging between the side of the road and Yurgen's barley field, juiced up as if she were in heat. Nevil was hopping ditches and fences after her, arms flailing like a crazy man, yelling to drown out Satan. Uncle Horace and Bjarne let the heifers frolic under my parents' watch and joined up with me and Yurgen.

The cow had doubled back on Nevil and was running at us. We split up and made a fence of ourselves. The cow was in hysterics by then, what with Nevil and the wind running her silly. When she saw us standing there she veered off, tried to jump a ditch and went down. She didn't get back up. It took us all a second to realize we had an injured cow on our hands, but when we did, the jocularity was replaced by another face of the crazy wind: panic. Yurgen ran like he was twenty again; I ran like I was fifty, tripping over everything, heart thumping as if it would break. Uncle Horace got there first and spit out a litany of swear words I didn't know he owned. Nevil caught up with the cow and stood panting and looking as if he were in pain. Bjarne crouched over the cow with Yurgen, one hand on Yurgen's shoulder. The cow was on her side, bellowing; one hind leg was bent under her at an impossible angle. "There's nothing for her," said Yurgen. "Martin, get the tractor. And the shotgun. Let's get the rest of these cows in the pasture."

There's yet another face of that crazy wind: sorrow. While we went about doing what we had to do, our innards churned the music-box lament of the bereaved. At the best of times the death of a beast will leave you limp, make you lose your appetite, make you feel sick to your stomach, and here we were all under the influence of the weather. We stumbled around as if the devil had come and taken our souls. Bjarne and Uncle Horace drove the heifers into the far pasture. It was easy now; the heifers themselves moved as if drugged. Yurgen stayed with the injured cow, stroking her neck, and when I came back with the gun and the front end loader, my father volunteered to administer the one shot between the cow's eyes and to slit her throat. The injured cow was 223, one of Yurgen's best milkers, which gave a heifer every year. The shot was to stun her; the knife to the throat was to bleed the life from her.

We chained the carcass up to the front end loader by the back legs, hoisted her up and took her back to the farm. There's nothing as gruesome as a cow before she's skinned. After she's skinned she's just another steak. But hanging up by her back legs like that — bouncing with every movement of the tractor, her throat slit and her head hanging backwards, eyes clouded over and tongue hanging out — well, that's the picture of death.

I parked Yurgen's tractor behind his barn, close to the

pasture fence, and let the loader down so the cow was almost lying flat. Skinning a cow is a little like taking off long underwear. You cut around the hocks — there isn't much meat around the lower legs — and slice from hock to groin and from groin to brisket, all the while cutting the skin away from fat and flesh. The farther down you skin, the higher the cow should hang. Nevil raised the bucket of the front end loader now and again, as Bjarne instructed, and I mostly stood around and watched; my dad, Bjarne and Uncle Horace were in there scraping the hide off the cow under my mother's direction; Yurgen was hunting in his tool shed for the meat saw.

Once the head was cut off, and most of the skinning was done, Uncle Horace cut around the genitals and sliced down the stomach from groin to neck. A cow's stomach is big, like a forty-five-gallon drum, and once the genital area is detached, the guts and uterus slide out like jelly and snakes.

Nevil hoisted the cow up completely and backed the tractor away from the pile of head, guts and reproductive organs. Yurgen and Uncle Horace finished skinning her, and Horace started cutting her in half, from groin to neck, with the meat saw.

Bjarne Lindskoog had been my 4-H leader and he never stopped teaching me; he was the area AI expert then, before it was routine for farmers to do their own inseminating. He went from farm to farm sticking tubes of prize-winning frozen bull sperm into the uteri of cows, his arm disappearing up to the shoulder, leaving the cow forever longing for the excitement of a good bull. Artificial insemination was a skill I was destined to learn from Bjarne. Bjarne knew everything you ever wanted to know about a cow's reproductive tract.

Looking over what was left of Yurgen's cow, Bjarne said, "You ever seen where the babies come from?" I shook my head and jammed my hands further into my pockets. Bjarne pointed at the heap of guts. "Yah, so this here's the ovaries," said Bjarne. "Little egg baskets." He pointed at two things that looked like wet plums. "And this here's what you call your cervix. Just like a turkey neck. Feel it." I dutifully felt it. "And that is the uterus, baby's home." He pointed out a sack; it looked very much like the stomach. "Yah, so this one, she's pregnant. Long ways along."

"Seven months," said Yurgen. "Always dropped a heifer." Nevil, sitting in the tractor, covered his face.

Bjarne pointed at the uterus. "This big horn's where the baby is and this little horn's where it isn't."

"If there were twins?" I said.

"If there were twins, yah, so this little horn is where the other would be. You want to see?" I'd seen plenty of calves, even premature ones, but there's always that perverse pleasure in seeing the unborn. I nodded. Bjarne sliced open the sack. Watery liquid rushed out and then the calf; it was dead, of course, a heifer, and didn't look much different from the calves I'd pulled live so many times, only much smaller, about three-quarters the size; such tiny feet. "These here are buttons," said Bjarne and pointed out little bulges on the inside of the sack. "The cotyledon."

"Cottledown," I said, trying to get the word.

"Yah," said Bjarne. "And this is where the placenta attaches to the wall of the uterus, on these buttons."

"Plus centa," I said.

"So," said Bjarne, "sperm — bull's hiccup juice — "

"Hiccup juice," I said.

"Goes to the vagina," he said, and pointed at the cow's disembodied genitalia lying in the grass. "Up the turkey neck, to the uterus where it meets the egg from the basket." He pointed at the plums. "And you got this baby."

"Turkey neck," I said. Clear as day.

By now Uncle Horace had finished sawing the carcass, and it was past suppertime. Uncle Horace, I think, was glad for an excuse to head home, even if it meant he had to stop off at Ed Hammerstein's butcher shop to get there, so he volunteered to take the carcass over to Ed's. We spread out plastic sheets on the bed of Uncle Horace's truck and loaded on the meat. He drove off and Ella came out to invite the rest of us in for coffee. What remained of cow 223 was left where it was, for crow bait.

We all slapped our hats on our pants and knocked the mud off our boots outside, and tried to rub away some of the grime with our hankies when we shrugged our way into the parlour. The Zurbeens' house had been built right into their barn, in the old Dutch way, by Henk who'd died some years before. The room where we were taking our coffee was a milking parlour come winter. The floor was covered with boards and carpet, and the walls were whitewashed and hung with some of Ella's paintings, and you wouldn't have noticed it was a milking parlour if you didn't know it, except for the water line connections and a couple of spigots at hip level in the walls. Only thing much different was the divided wood door at the far end of the room from the fireplace; it led into the barn. We arranged ourselves in a half-circle around the fireplace to take our coffee. I remember looking out the window and thinking it had suddenly turned hellishly dark; rain had started sliding down the window, and lightning flashed now and again. The disappointment over the cow was showing on Yurgen's face. He never said much, but what he didn't say — approval, disapproval, sorrow, pride — was printed on his face clear as the billboards at Hobbema. He had a nose like a rooster's beak, and would have a good crop of hair even into his nineties. He's one of those men who wears a beard without looking shaggy; if he wasn't, Ella would've got him to shave quick enough. She's not a pushy woman, but she gets her way; you know by the way they keep touching each other.

Ella floated from kitchen to parlour, making coffee, serving cakes, disappearing, reappearing, her skirt rustling like poplar leaves. Mom tried to help but got shooed out of the kitchen.

"It's a sad thing to lose a cow," said my father.

"Yah, it's sad to lose a cow," said Bjarne. "But when you lose a calf, that hurts."

Nevil looked miserable, so I got the conversation flowing in another direction. "You hear about the freemartins?" I said. Of course, everybody in that cow parlour had heard about them. About two years before, a cow belonging to a dairyman in Wetaskiwin had given birth — remarkably — to four calves in one birthing, two freemartins and two bull calves. A freemartin is a heifer calf born as a twin with a bull calf. Hormones from the bull calf affect the developing heifer within the womb, and the freemartin is often born missing parts of her reproductive tract. She's bully. A freemartin is no good to the cattleman or the dairyman. She'll never give birth, so she'll never give milk. "Now one of the freemartins is milking," I said. "You believe that? She's milking."

"I've seen stranger things," said Yurgen, and everybody turned to him. He sucked at his pipe.

"What kinda things you seen?" said Lindskoog.

"Just things," said Yurgen.

I looked over at Nevil and he looked back at me. "I've got something strange," said Nevil, and he pulled from his pocket the weird glass ball his mother kept on her fireplace mantle. Lately Nevil had taken to snitching the ball and carrying it around with him. He said he saw things in it.

Yurgen slipped the pipe from his mouth and stared at the thing. My mother took the ball from Nevil and held it up to the light. We lost her there for a moment to some daydream, then she shook herself out of it.

"Well," said my mother. "Let me tell you about this thing." And she told us a story that happened long before I was born. There were many details I filled in for myself later — details I gleaned from my father, from Aunt Marion, from Mrs. Shute — things I couldn't wrangle from my mother. What my mother did tell us flushed and excited her; she spoke quickly and breathlessly like a girl describing her first love. I don't know why my mother chose this spring night, in the unlikely setting of Zerbeen's cow parlour, to tell her story. It was so out of character for her to admit passion in this way. But then, we'd just run with cows that played like heifers, and looked death in the face. Blame it on the crazy wind.

It had all happened the year of the silage towers. Uncle Horace and my father had built identical wooden silage towers with their last name, "Winkle," written along the tops in identical black lettering. At the time, in 1951, having a silo, much less a personalized silo, was an extravagance. They'd contracted the towers separately from the same company during the same spring, and when Horace, being the eldest brother, came over to check out a bull my father had for sale, and saw Dad had the exact same lettering, and in black, of "Winkle" along the top of his tower, he turned on his heel and marched back home over two miles of dusty road, so angry he forgot he'd driven the truck to my father's farm. He sent Aunt Marion to pick up the Ford. My dad and Horace didn't talk to each other all spring after that incident.

That spring — the spring of the silage towers — my mother became pregnant for the first time, with Louise. It was a late pregnancy, in that Mom was almost thirty. For all those concerned — even Horace — it was a relief. Marion carried the news home like a proud cat and Horace, despite himself, smiled. "About time," he said and patted the head of his own eldest boy, Timothy, then almost eleven, starting to shoot up and right handy on the tractor.

It'd been touch and go whether Mom and Dad — or rather, Elsie and Enfred, they weren't my parents yet — would ever have a child to help them on the farm, to be security for their old age. They'd been doing their best to propagate for going on ten years and nothing had caught. Enfred had even gone through the shameful fertility test like some useless bull but, the Lord is merciful, he checked out okay. Just before the pregnancy Enfred had even come to suspect Elsie wasn't fertile, or worse, maybe Elsie didn't want a child. Maybe she was protecting herself, secretly. The thought was torture. In a fit of helpless self-pity (after seeing Horace and his two sons at a distance sitting on their tractor steps eating lunch and laughing), Enfred had shuffled through the contents of Elsie's purse, looked into the recesses of the kitchen cupboards and into her underwear drawer. But no, there were no tubes or concoctions, only a few old love letters he'd written when she'd spent that year at college, and three bars of Cuban Lunch.

In despair he sat on their bed clutching a pair of Elsie's underwear, blindly eating all three Cuban Lunches. Of course Elsie came in just then, dressed in her work overalls, and in sock feet. She smelled like the dairy barn, but then so did Enfred.

"What?" she said.

"I?" said Enfred.

And so Elsie and Enfred stopped talking to each other, although Enfred wasn't sure why and Elsie couldn't bring herself to say a thing, such was her embarrassment over the chocolate bars, her anger at having her privacy violated. Elsie cooked silent dinners and they ate in silence. They did the chores together in silence, although here the silence was eased by the thumping of the milk pumps and water sprays, the shoosh of the grain shoots, and the bawling of the cows. For a week they did not make love, so solid was their silence.

Then Enfred's cows, on the north pasture, broke into Horace's barley field. Horace's crop was at dough stage, just two weeks to swathing, and the bloody stupid cows feasted until they were sick. Enfred spotted the cows loose on Horace's field on the way home from town, and after parking the truck lopsided in the yard and yelling for Elsie to come out and help, ran across the field to the cows in his town clothes. Elsie caught up to him, and together they brought home the cows. Cow 39, or Old Nelly as Elsie called her, was so sick she could hardly move. Enfred called in Oscar Podritski, the vet, and by the time Oscar arrived, Nelly was lying in the barnyard on her side; her belly was so big you'd have thought she was birthing twins.

"We'll have to do a rumenectomy," said Oscar.

"Cut her open?" said Enfred.

"That's what I said," said Oscar.

So Nelly's belly was shaved, anaesthetized and sliced open, the layers of fat and muscle pulled back and her gut opened. Oscar scooped out handful after handful of mulched green barley, and the pile of it beside Nelly finally measured three feet by three feet. Oscar stuffed the stomach, muscle and fat back into place, sewed her up and wrote out his bill. Nelly belched. Enfred did the chores alone that night. Elsie stayed beside Nelly for a time, shooing away cats and keeping flies off. It was then she saw the little ball in the pile of Nelly's stomach contents, shining in the barnyard light like gold. Elsie picked it out of the muck, ran it under water from the outside tap and rubbed it on her jack-shirt. It looked like glass, but it didn't somehow. When she held the ball up to the light, Elsie saw everything around her in that ball, even what was behind her. It was as if the ball contained their farm within itself, or rather, as if the ball contained the whole world, for wasn't that Horace and Marion's farm she saw as well? And over there George and Gilda s place? But it couldn't be; when she took her eye away from the ball and looked in the direction of Horace and Marion's farm, all she saw was dark.

Elsie sat on the stool next to the cow and looked and looked into the ball. Each time she looked she swore she saw another part of the neighbourhood. There was Likely, the Hotel, the Cafe; there was Lamentations Church. There was her parents' home, freshly painted as it had been when she was a little girl, long before her parents died. There was the cat named Andy Gump who had slept on her bed every night until it was killed by her father's truck. And there was a little red-haired girl holding the cat; it wasn't Elsie, no, but it could have been, she seemed so familiar, the resemblance was so great. Elsie searched her mind for a memory of this little girl, but found no one. Of course every time she took her eye away she swore she couldn't have seen these things.

"Where'd this thing come from?" asked Enfred, when he and Elsie finally sat down for coffee at the kitchen table. When Enfred held the ball up to the light, he saw the old house where he'd grown up, about ten miles up the road, the barn where he'd bottle-fed his first calf, a calf his father had insisted on slaughtering, as a lesson in living. And there was the prize Ayrshire — best milker in his father's herd — that his father had promised Enfred and, forgetting, given to Horace; the cow had died within a year of being in Horace's care, and Enfred had been glad. But of course when Enfred took his eye away he realized he couldn't have seen these things. "A trick of light," he said.

When Elsie looked at the ball again in this warmer inside light, she saw her aunt's home with its lace-covered table, and look! there was the parlour with the plates of iced cakes and the dolls with ceramic faces. There was her aunt smiling, waving in her odd way, like a church choir director, elegant, Victorian. But of course this, too, was impossible. Her aunt had died years ago, and the house had burned down during that year of bad wind storms. "It's the oddest thing," said Elsie.

"Weird," said Enfred. "Put the thing away. Let's get some sleep." Enfred scratched his hair into a haystack and made his way to the bedroom, throwing his overalls and jack-shirt, his jeans and socks, to the floor as he went. Elsie took another look into the ball and saw the library of the Prairie Bible Institute where she'd gone for that year, and the boy she'd met there — his shirt ironed, his hair neatly combed, his fingernails clean — waving for her to come over. She saw her room at the college, and the girl named Shelly she'd shared it with laughing and laughing, as if Elsie had just told a joke. Elsie forced herself to stop looking at the ball and nested it in some wool on a plate on the kitchen table, covering it as if to keep it warm.

The next day Marion came over at coffee time. Enfred greeted her but went out to work on fencing, leaving his coffee half-drunk.

"How's Enfred?" said Marion.

"Okay, I guess."

"Not getting along so well?"

"Not so well as all that," said Elsie, but in that way that let Marion know she wasn't going to talk about it. "Cows got into your barley field yesterday," she said. "Oscar came out and opened up Nelly because she ate too much. Found this inside." Elsie pulled the ball from under the wool and held it up. In the morning light it looked green.

"Well," said Marion.

"When you put it up to the light you see the most amazing things. Wish I knew what it was. Want to take a look?"

"No, no, I don't think so," said Marion. "Got to get home to the kids. Can't leave them too long unattended; they keep a woman busy." Marion winked. "You'll be knowing about that soon enough, I expect."

Elsie felt her stomach sink. But she smiled and put the ball in her apron pocket and walked Marion to the door. Marion turned and put her hand on Elsie's arm. "Why don't you take that ball to Mrs. Zachariuk?" she said. "She might know what it is."

That afternoon as Elsie and Enfred drove into town, they stopped in on Mrs. Zachariuk. Mrs. Zachariuk was mother to Mrs. Shute — Julie Zachariuk had become Mrs. Nevil Shute just the winter before, after marrying that banker against her mother's wishes. Mrs. Zachariuk was the last surviving member of the only Ukrainian family ever to live in Likely. Like her own mother, Mrs. Zachariuk had been converted by members of the Methodist mission at the turn of the century, but like her mother she found no reason to give up many of the Greek Orthodox practices, and that made her as magical and foreign and suspect, to our German Baptist community, as the Pope. Nevertheless, Mrs. Zachariuk was known for the mammoth size of the vegetables she grew, the wonder of her cooking and the strength of her uncanny wisdom. It was assumed that she was a witch, an assumption borne up by the fact that in the early days of Likely she'd added to her husband's meagre farm income by offering her services as midwife. She was getting on, that spring of the silage towers, and a year later she would begin to die; her memories would gradually leave her until there was nothing of Mrs. Zachariuk left.

That day Mrs. Zachariuk took the ball from Elsie, rolled it in her hands, held it up to window light and looked through it, put it in her mouth and rolled her eyes. She took the ball from her mouth and put it in her apron pocket.

"You, Fred," she said. "Track that dirt back out of here. I'll talk to your woman alone."

Enfred looked at Elsie, shrugged and went to wait in the truck. Mrs. Zachariuk's face went all of a sudden soft. She smiled and took Elsie's wrist, put the glass ball in Elsie's hand and squeezed it shut. "You put this under your pillow and your love will sing," she said. "It'll sing with all the children you wish for." Mrs. Zachariuk winked.

"What is it?" said Elsie.

"It doesn't matter. Don't concern yourself. It won't harm you. Only good comes of it."

"But how did the cow get it?" said Elsie.

Mrs. Zachariuk shrugged. "Where did the cow find it?"

"She was eating on Horace and Marion's field," said Elsie.

"Maybe you should go ask Marion."

Back in the cow parlour, Ella Zerbeen refilled all our cups as my mother told the last of her story. "Did you ask Aunt Marion?" I said.

"No, I never asked Marion," said Mom. "I never told anybody about it. They'd think I was crazy. You all probably think I'm crazy."

Everyone shifted and mumbled, "No, no, you're not crazy."

"Didn't Mrs. Zachariuk say any more about it?" said Bjarne. "Where the thing came from?"

"No, nothing at all. After Louise was conceived, I took the ball back to Mrs. Zachariuk and I guess it stayed in that house until Nevil here got a hold of it."

"Who was the girl in the ball?" said Ella. "The red-haired girl?"

"That was Louise," said my mother. "Imagine! I saw her even before she was conceived."

No one commented on that. Louise was still a sore spot in our household; the summer before she and Russell Schmidt had taken Russell's pickup to Edmonton and gotten married by a justice of the peace. They came back to Likely to live in a used trailer on one of Russell's father's pastures. We didn't see much of Louise for a while.

My mother handed the ball back to Nevil. He held it in his lap and stared at it.

"How about you, Yurgen?" said Lindskoog. "What do you know about that ball?"

"Nothing that pays a man to talk about," said Yurgen. He sucked on his pipe and the room went quiet, and then one of Yurgen and Ella's cows, a pet they had named Molly, forced open the door at the end of the room and bawled. "Yurgen," said Ella. "She only does that when she's about to calve."

All of us except Nevil clambered out the parlour door and into the barn with our cups of coffee. We stood around Molly, pulling on her calf's legs, laughing at the calf's tongue licking away when his eyes weren't even passed out of the old cow yet, pulling the mucus from the beastie's nose, handing out advice that was neither good nor bad nor new. Through the fly-dirt on the barn window I saw Nevil walking, the crazy wind whipping at his jacket, out to the low rise of the coulee. He pitched something over the coulee bank, into Lindskoog's field, something that caught the light like a star and vanished. The rain hit the tin roof like bullets; steam came off the calf, off our coffee cups, out of our mouths. Old Ella leaned at the doorway to the parlour in her pretty Sunday apron with her arms folded, and grinned at us like we were kids.

FATHERS, SONS AND HIRED HANDS

THE fitness craze jogged right by Likely and kept on going until it hit Edmonton. Jogging was a secular activity akin to dancing; all those sweaty bodies and tight clothes and, in particular, the jigging. The one exception was Al MacLean. Al was one of the city folks who had moved to Likely to take advantage of the cheap land and houses. Like the others, he commuted to his job in Edmonton, where he was a bank manager, but he spent his evenings and weekends jogging the streets of Likely. Al had read somewhere that you should pace yourself by carrying on a conversation as you jogged. As he had no jogging partner, he carried on conversations with himself, and that pretty much set him apart from the lifelong residents of Likely. At first Al discussed politics with himself as he ran, but as it was difficult to maintain an interesting conversation about politics without a little heated debate, he soon sought out other topics to keep himself occupied. He jogged circuits around horseshoe-shaped Centre Avenue and talked about the winning streak the Oilers were on, how hard it was to find a parking place in Edmonton and how God-awful expensive it was to get a suit dry-cleaned those days.

Things like jogging were expected of bank managers. But for the rest of us, jogging was looked upon as a sinful use of spare time. For the members of Lamentations Church, the approved way to spend your spare time ran along the lines of building churches — or starting them, at any rate. As none of the farmers really had much spare time, any community project that took longer than a weekend was pretty much doomed from the start. The very first Lamentations Church was started near the railway tracks around 1920, when the community was expanding. But that project petered out around the time of the Great Depression. Pastor Gottlieb got everyone all steamed up there for a while in the midsixties about getting a new church built. Land was even purchased for that purpose and a foundation laid, on the other side of the coulee from Lindskoog's, but enthusiasm for the project ran out when Pierre Trudeau came into power like the anti-Christ himself. Why would anyone bother building a church when the end was near? So instead the Lamentations congregation rented out the old dance hall from Wallace Hammerstein, rolled in the baptismal tank, and waited.

The world didn't end, however, and in 1974, with a year left in their lease at the dance hall, members of the church board started talking themselves into starting up the building project again.

"The hall roof needs work," said Rudy Bierlie. "That rainfall last Sunday ruined Mrs. Mulder's hat."

"It's in the contract: the church will do repairs," said Wallace Hammerstein.

"And that's another thing," said Uncle Horace. "We're paying for a lot of things you don't usually pay for when you're renting."

"We can't go on forever baptising in a dance hall," said

Rudy. "This was supposed to be a temporary place, till we got the new church built."

"But the cost," said Wallace Hammerstein.

"Yah, so finishing that building would save us plenty in the long run," said Lindskoog. "What with the rent we wouldn't be paying you."

"Here, here," said Uncle Horace.

"I don't think we can afford to leave the construction for another year," said Rudy. "We've got half a building standing out there, rotting. We've just got to find the time to finish the thing."

So it was decided. The men of Lamentations Church would gather at least one day each weekend until that church was built, right after planting season was through and school let out. Of course, by the time next summer rolled around, the will to complete the new church had gone dry once again. Wallace had already rented the dance hall to the Anglicans, but he was able to let the congregation rent the building that had housed Ed's Butchery and Car Repair the year before, when Ed Hammerstein was alive and things were better for him. The new church was a square brick building characteristic of Alberta architecture of the 1920s and befitting the austere aspirations of the Lamentations brethren. The men of the church did their best to renovate the interior of the building — over the course of a weekend — by painting the walls, the pews and the old stock tank white. But the scent of raw meat and petrol lingered, like ghosts of past prosperity.

As everyone in Likely knew, the ghost of Ed himself occasionally haunted the new church. Aunt Gilda said he came to her while she was in the church office typing up the Sunday program. Ed gestured wildly and opened his mouth as if he were talking. But Aunt Gilda couldn't make out a thing he said, so she told him where the bathroom was now and, as he seemed satisfied with that, she went back to her typing.

That sighting was borne out by another story, told by Rudy Bierlie, our one-legged shop teacher, of a man wearing white coveralls covered in black and red hand prints who appeared by the old stock tank that served as our baptismal tank. The apparition looked up, saw Rudy, took a step back, tripped over his shoelaces and disappeared. He knew it was Ed, Rudy said, because Ed never could tie his shoelaces.

Ed's demise was an interesting one, as Likely deaths went: it was unplanned. Almost everyone in Likely had the forethought to let their neighbours know they were going to get sick or die. You knew someone was about to get sick when they said in passing, "I've been feeling a little tired lately." That was the signal to cook up an extra batch of squares and hustle over to the invalid's to help them out with chores. If someone said, "I've been feeling so tired I just haven't been able to get any work done," then that was when you rustled the invalid into Camrose for some medical attention and worked out a volunteer schedule of women to help the family out with cooking and household tasks, if the invalid was a woman, or a schedule of men to help out with field work and chores, if the invalid was a man. If a man said, "Well, it's time to sell the farm and move into town," that was when you started preparing a eulogy.

Ed's death, on the other hand, came as a surprise. He had died the summer before the congregation moved out of the dance hall. He was taking Mrs. Shute's powder-blue '72 Duster for a test drive down the highway, trying to figure out what that noise was, when the brakes failed and Ed and the car smacked right into a power pole. Accidents were frowned on in Likely. A more accepted way to die was from exhaustion; there were a lot of farmers slowly killing themselves that way, with overwork. It wasn't a foolproof method, though. Able Hammerstein, Ed and Wallace's father, had been trying to overwork himself to death most of his life, and he was still going strong.

Ed Hammerstein, Able's younger son, made his living as a mechanic and butcher, but like almost everyone in Likely, he dabbled in raising beef. He rented, from his father, a section of land that backed onto the town of Likely itself and pastured cattle on it. Ed didn't bother building a barn to shelter his beasts; he used the Texas house. Able's father, Clyde, had come up to Alberta during the big immigration of U.S. citizens to the province, seen in the countryside the possibility of profit, and moved both his wife, Emma, and his house up from Texas. Clyde's claim to fame was a pet monkey that had the run of the house and pretty much made a mess of it, but even back then the Hammersteins had money and they hired one of the local women, Bjarne Lindskoog's great-aunt, to clean up after the monkey, among other things. Able was Clyde Hammerstein's only son, and when Clyde died within a year of Emma's death, the house and farm all went to him. Clyde and Emma were buried on the farm behind their home according to their wishes, beside their pet monkey, who had died some years before. But the old Texas house stayed empty until Ed's cows moved in. Able and his father had had a falling out over the use of a piece of land that was never settled, and after Clyde's death Able refused to move into his father's house. Wallace Hammerstein and his bride, Evangeline, had wanted a brand-new house, and Ed was content living in the back of his mechanic's shop. Much of the house was beyond repair in any case, and it got worse once Ed's cows moved in. The cows frequently knocked down the doors of the Texas house, but never busted them, and Ed just put them back on with new hinges. They don't make doors like that any more.

It was an embarrassment, seeing those cows mosey in and out of the house like guests come over for iced tea, and we had to explain it to any newcomer to Likely, as the house was plainly visible past Wallace Hammerstein's tractor dealership. But this wasn't what got everybody mad at Ed. It was that one of his cows kept getting out and walking down Centre Avenue, leaving evidence of her passage on the gravel roads that passed for streets. Most Saturday mornings at the Cafe, it was all there was to talk about.

"That cow's a genuine fence-crawler," said Dad.

"A cow like that you got to keep in a board fence," said Lindskoog. "But you got to make sure she don't get out through the knot-holes."

Mom, Dad and I were sitting in the Cafe with Rudy Bierlie, Bjarne Lindskoog and Nevil Shute, my best friend, drinking coffee and eating lemon pie that wasn't near as good as my mother's, everyone agreed. Outside the Cafe window, Ed's cow — we knew her by the streak of white running from one end of her backbone to the other — was ambling down the street sniffing windows and licking doorknobs. As we watched, she walked through Harry Wyton's open door right into the General Store and licked the ice-cream freezer.

Seeing that, Lindskoog started to grumble about Ed's ability as a cattleman. "Yah, he don't feed those cows right," he said.

"Imagine keeping them in a house," said my mother.

"Poor pasture management all round," said Rudy Bierlie. He said this with some guilt, because his own pasture hadn't been worked properly for a decade and we all knew it.

The cow backed out of the General Store, and Harry

Wyton came out after her and locked the door behind him. Harry was about the only man in town who didn't know cows, and he didn't really mind Ed's cow getting out so much. Harry got precious little opportunity to herd cows, and he read enough westerns to believe it was still a romantic thing to do. While the cow stood there watching him, Harry got in his pickup, started it and began turning circles around the cow. She stared at him for a moment or two, sniffing the ground, then started running and kicking up her heels. Of course a cow chased with a pickup only panics, goes running off in all directions, so Harry pretty much tore up Centre Avenue over the weeks with his attempts at herding. His starting and stopping left ruts everywhere.

Lindskoog shook his head and said, "He's going to kill that cow."

Al, the bank manager, jogged by the open Cafe door, explaining his bank's policy on late loan payments. My dad sighed, and he and Lindskoog got up and walked outside. My mom gave me and Nevil a look, and we got up to help as well. Lindskoog put his hand up so Harry would stop his truck. Once the cow had calmed down a little, the four of us walked her back to the Texas house pasture with relatively little fuss.

While he was closing the gate to the pasture, my father said to me, "Go tell Ed his cow was out again."

"Why don't you tell him?" I said.

"Because I told you to do it," he said.

I grumbled for a bit for Nevil's benefit, and then Nevil and I went over to Ed Hammerstein's shop, where we found Ed lying under the professor guy's red Toyota.

"Ed, your cow's out again," I said.

Ed didn't bother to come out from under the car. "I'll get right on it," he said.

"We put her in for you," I said.

"Thanks," he said.

Nevil and I stared at Ed's boots for a while. They weren't tied then either.

"You should do something," I said. "To keep her in."

"I'll get right on it," he said. "You can count on it."

Nevil and I left Ed and went for ice cream and Orange Crush at the General Store. That summer Nevil and I were both sixteen, and Nevil had been my friend forever. When we were maybe nine or ten, we pretended to be the men who would someday walk on the moon. My father's dairy parlour with all its tubes and switches was our spaceship. I put on my father's netted beekeeper's hat for a space helmet and Nevil and I walked real slow because of the heavy suits, like deep-sea divers' suits. We sang, "Moon shines bright on Mary Cartright, she can't fart right, her ass is airtight."

It was Nevil, too, who offered me my first profound moment. We were standing with our backs against the warm school wall, looking over the playing field, with our shoes and socks off, and wiggling our toes in the grass, even though Mrs. Noyes forbade us to take off our shoes. Nevil said, "You know how you're walking and you get a rock in your shoe and then you take it out and you keep on walking like you got a rock in your shoe?"

"Yeah," I said, with surprise and wonder, and for that moment the world made sense.

But Nevil had grown into a tall, slim and sharp-nosed young man who didn't know a thing about cars or football or hockey, and worse, didn't care. In Likely that was a social liability. Worse yet, for me, Nevil didn't try to avoid trouble; he stood up to people when they did bad things. Just before school ended for the summer, Wally Hammerstein Junior and his buddies taped a sheet of paper that said "wide load" on Dorothy Slabie's back, and she went around all morning, unknowingly, like that. Nevil walked up to Wally right in the middle of the lunch-hour football game and said, "What do you get out of doing stuff like that?"

Everybody stopped playing and stood around watching. Nevil looked around and turned red, but he went on talking anyway. "What is it with you? Why can't you treat other people with respect?"

I figured this was something he must have picked up from his mother, who was reading a lot of self-help books at the time.

Wally Hammerstein Junior smirked and said, "Listen to Snivelling Nevil, everybody. He wants some respect."

From then on, of course, everybody called him Snivelling Nevil. Not content to leave well enough alone, Nevil went to Camrose and got a T-shirt made that said "Snivelling Nevil" and wore it to school. When I saw him in it, I said, "That's going to cause trouble."

"Wally's a jerk," he said. "Somebody's got to stand up to him."

At noon Wally Hammerstein Junior and his buddies walked up to Nevil and me while we ate our lunches at a picnic table near the swings, watching kids play Frisbee on the field. Wally plucked Nevil up by the T-shirt and said, "Fag." Nevil made kissy noises at him, which I didn't think was wise. Wally dropped Nevil and Nevil went back to eating lunch. "What a fag," said Wally. "Bet you wear your mama's skirts, eh? Borrow her undies?"

The other guys laughed. Wally pushed me into Nevil and then called over to the kids playing Frisbee. "Hey, everybody," he said. "Look at the nice T-shirt Snivelling Nevil's wearing. He likes to be fashionable. He likes to wear his mother's dresses. This here's his sweetheart. Nevil loves Martin, Nevil loves Martin."

I wanted to sink into the grass and disappear. Instead I took my lunch bag and went into the school, leaving Nevil sitting there alone, eating his cheese sandwich in front of a school of laughing faces.

The next day Nevil came to school dressed in a kilt.

Well, if anyone hadn't been talking before, they were talking now. The following Saturday the adult crowd at the Cafe were gossiping about Nevil and his "tendencies." I heard them myself. I was sitting with Mom and Dad and Uncle Horace. Evangeline Hammerstein sat at the table behind us, talking about Nevil as if I weren't sitting right there. She said, "Well, naturally he'd go soft. He didn't have a male influence, did he? With his father dead."

Uncle Horace turned around and joined the conversation. He said, "He's one of them artist types. You could see it in him as a boy. All artist types naturally go fag. They can't help themselves."

My mother said, "Please!" loud enough that Evangeline and Uncle George looked at her. She eyed me and then eyed them, to tell them they should be ashamed of themselves. Uncle Horace turned back to our table and fiddled with his coffee cup. Al, the bank manager, jogged by the fly strips on the Cafe door humming the theme from *2001: A Space Odyssey*. Then Ed Hammerstein's cow wandered down the street and Evangeline started talking about how somebody should lock that cow up once and for all.

I had mixed feelings. Nevil was my best friend and I really did like the guy. But I was pretty low on the social scale myself, and I couldn't afford to go any lower. If I hung around Nevil too much everybody would come to think I was a fag, as they had already begun to do, and that would destroy my chances of ever getting a date.

As we watched Ed's cow dance down the street, my

father said, "Nevil just needs some hard work. A few callouses turn any boy into a man."

My mother said, "Well, why don't you hire Nevil on for the summer? You said yourself we need somebody, and we've left it so late."

My father had never hired help before; he had kids. But seeing as how Louise was pretty much disowned at the moment — she and Russel Schmidt were still living in a junky old trailer in the middle of a cow pasture owned by Russell's father, and Louise was working at Hay Lakes Cafe as a waitress — I was the only help remaining. Since he really didn't know how to go about it, Dad had left hiring very late, so the choices were down to Nevil or an old bachelor named Johanson who lived in a squatter's shack on the far side of Joe Lake; he was rumoured to take a bus up to Edmonton once a month to visit an old prostitute who'd long since retired from the labour force.

"Sure, we could hire Nevil," said my father. "Eh, Martin?"

"I don't want Nevil working for us," I said.

"Why not?" said my mother.

How could I explain? I thought of coming out with it; I thought of saying, "I'm trying to drop Nevil as a friend because everybody who thinks he's a fag picks on me," but then I'd get an hour-long lecture on Christian duty towards our fellow man, and how a Christian must suffer for his charity and so on. I said, "I just don't want him to."

"Well, he's going to work for us whether you want it or not," said my mother.

"Why? Why can't you get someone else?" I said.

"Because your father's the boss and he can hire who he wants," said Mom.

I drooped in my chair and ate from the tiny bowl of vanilla ice cream and stared out the Cafe window at Ed's cow eating the grass around a power pole.

Ice cream was one of the reasons I liked visiting Nevil's house so much. Mrs. Shute always served me a huge bowl when I showed up, as she did that Saturday, after I left my parents and Uncle Horace at the Cafe. I went over to ask Nevil if he wanted the job on our farm for the summer, as my mother had forced me to. Mrs. Shute filled up three soup bowls with strawberry ice cream covered in chocolate syrup, banana slices and whipped cream, and the three of us ate quickly and with gusto. Mrs. Shute had her hair tied back in a kerchief, and she wore jeans and runners. This was her Saturday outfit, her relief from a work week of high heels and blouses with bow-ties. Nevil wore jeans and a striped T-shirt.

"I told Dad I figured you wouldn't be interested," I said. "But Dad said to ask anyway. You'd be cleaning shit out of the calf barn, loading up hay, stuff like that. I found maggots in the calf stall last Saturday when I cleaned them out. Sometimes the calves get the shits and you have to clean up this yellow runny stuff. Some calves get these huge, pussy abscesses under their chins. You got to stick a needle full of iodine into the puss and, when you do that, puss squirts out all over you. It's really gross."

"Well, what do you think?" said Mrs. Shute.

"Sure," said Nevil. "I need the bucks. I'll camp over some nights. We'll go fishing. It'll be great."

That was it, then. Nevil would work for us and Wally would convince the school I was a fag, because he said Nevil was a fag. I would be guilty by association.

Mrs. Shute said to me, "I hear you've been having some trouble with Wally again." I spooned up the last of my ice cream and didn't say anything, because I knew my face had given me away. "Don't be afraid to stand up to him," said

Mrs. Shute. "He's a big scared boy. More scared than you can imagine."

I shrugged and Nevil punched me in the shoulder, an invitation to wrestle. I pushed him off his chair and we roughhoused through the kitchen into the living room.

I left Nevil and Mrs. Shute's house and headed to the General Store, where I'd said I'd meet my father. Wally and his buddies crossed the street from Hammerstein's tractor dealership and came up behind me. "Been visiting your boyfriend?" said Wally.

He pinched my butt and said, "Ooo." I ignored him at first, as Mrs. Shute had suggested, and kept walking, but Wally and his goons surrounded me, all limp wrists and swaying hips, saying, "Martin, oh, Martin," in falsetto voices. I finally pushed Wally away, but he pushed me back, hard, against the wall of the General Store and knocked the wind out of me.

"Fag," he said, and they walked off laughing.

The following Friday, with school over, Nevil came to work for us. The odd thing about farm work is that if you get paid for doing it, you take a dive on the social scale. On the social scale, paid help is slightly lower than kids. After years of watching and assimilating, after years of doing as I was told, I got it into my head that Nevil was obliged to do whatever I asked of him.

"Martin," said my father, over breakfast Friday morning. "You get those calf stalls cleaned out this afternoon. They're a disgrace."

When Nevil turned up for work that day I said, "You get those calf stalls cleaned up this afternoon. They're a disgrace."

Nevil shrugged and grinned and leaned on his pitchfork like Ken Dryden leaned on his hockey stick in front of the net, and that made me mad. "Your dad wants me to clean out the hay shed," he said.

"Those calf stalls too," I said. "They've got to be done this afternoon."

Nevil shrugged and smiled, and went off and forked old hay from the shed onto the hay rack. Come afternoon the calf stalls were still dirty. "You didn't clean out those calf stalls," I said.

"Your dad asked me to clean out the shed today," said Nevil. "I haven't finished."

I marched off to the calf barn and shovelled out the stalls quicker than I'd ever shovelled them before, I was so mad. By the time I was done cleaning them, the anger had dissipated into sheepishness. But I didn't say I was sorry. I hid in the barn until I knew it was time for Mrs. Shute to come pick Nevil up. I sat up in the hay loft, with my back against a bale of hay and my legs stretched out, and I drifted off, and when I woke a tomcat was pissing on my leg.

Of course I had to face Nevil the next morning, Saturday. He was sitting with Lindskoog on a pile of lumber near the unfinished church when Mom, Dad and I drove up. He was wearing his "Snivelling Nevil" T-shirt again. He lifted his chin to me so I had to talk to him. I said "Hi," and we walked off a little ways. The men who had already arrived stood around kicking dirt and chewing the fat. The women hustled back and forth from their cars to the two long tables set up near the half-finished church, putting out the coffee and food for the day.

"Why'd you have to wear that?" I said, pointing at his T-shirt.

Nevil shrugged and grinned.

"Everybody's talking like you're a fag, you know," I said.

He went red for a moment, and kicked dirt. "Let them talk. This town's full of yahoos."

"Wally pushes me around because of you," I said. "It's like you don't care. When you do this stuff, it affects me too."

"You know he's a jerk," said Nevil. "He pushes everyone around."

He elbowed me and I elbowed him back. He punched me in the shoulder and we wrestled on the grass for a while, until I saw Evangeline Hammerstein watching us. When I caught her eye, she turned, got in her car and drove off. I stood up and brushed off my jeans.

This was the first weekend of construction, so there was a good turnout. Every man from the congregation was there, including Wallace Hammerstein, who almost never left his dealership on a business day, and even Ed Hammerstein, who was rarely seen at social gatherings. But then community construction projects in Likely were what Saturday dances were to other communities; they were social events. The Ladies of Lamentations had laid out a feast of sandwiches, soups, coffee and squares, so all morning and into the afternoon the men of Lamentations got in more eating and gossiping than actual construction.

Just after lunch, Able Hammerstein barrelled down the road on his Minneapolis Moline tractor, throwing up dust that made everyone cough. He drove his tractor right up to Ed and Wallace who, together, were carting a board over to the construction site.

"Why's your shop closed?" said Able to Ed.

Ed grinned and shrugged.

"And why did you leave the dealership in the hands of that woman?" said Able to Wallace.

"The place is Evangeline's too," said Wallace. "I'm taking a day off."

"Saturday's the best business day," said Able. "What the hell are you slacking off for?"

"We're not slacking off," said Wallace. "We're building a church."

"You two got responsibilities!" said Able. "My phone's been ringing off the hook all morning. Carl Schmidt said he came all the way in for a part for his tractor. Evangeline didn't know what the hell he needed and now he's got to waste the whole day sitting around in the Cafe. And you! That professor guy wants to know where the hell his car is. You said he'd have it today."

Ed turned a little, red-faced, to look at his father, but as he did, he stepped on his own shoelace and tripped, lost his grip on the board and fell forward. Wallace leapt back, but the board came down on his foot so hard he yelled out.

My mother and several other Ladies of Lamentations said, "You all right?" But Wallace didn't answer. He turned on his heel, limped down the road his father had just stormed up and didn't stop limping until he reached Lindskoog's corn field a mile down the road.

We all watched, meanwhile, as Ed stood listening to his father rant. Ed kicked dirt, crossed his arms and looked over at the rest of us. Occasionally he nodded at his father, and then looked off at the sky.

"You hearing what I'm saying?" said Able.

"Yup," said Ed.

"You go right back to that shop, right now, and fix that professor guy's car. Today. Do you understand me?"

"I'll get right on it," said Ed. "You can count on it."

Able nodded once, gruffly, as if things were settled. He started up his tractor and sped back to town, choking us all once again with dust. Ed took off his cap, scratched his head, smiled shyly at us and went back to hammering. It was another week before the professor guy saw his red Toyota.

Not that any of us cared. In the year since he had bought

a house in Likely, the professor guy had never introduced himself to any of us, never even nodded in greeting. Local gossip had it that he worked in Edmonton, at the University of Alberta, and when we passed him on the street he looked stiffly ahead, as if he were in the city. It was the professor guy and Al MacLean who organized the meeting at Al's house for "concerned homeowners" who were upset about Harry Wyton's pickup tearing up the streets of Likely. I was in the General Store with Mom, picking out a chocolate bar, when Al and the professor guy, representing half a dozen city people, marched in. Harry was sitting behind the checkout counter reading *Bullets in My Teeth*, the fast-action sequel to *Knives in My Boots*, when they came in. He grudgingly put down the book and said, "How can I help you folks?"

"You can stop ripping up the streets with that truck of yours," said Al.

Harry's face went red, and he looked from one man to the other, then glanced around the store to see who was listening. He saw my mother looking at him from the vegetable cooler and went redder.

"I was just rounding up the cattle," said Harry.

"The cow," said Al. "One cow."

"I'm just being a good citizen," said Harry. "Somebody's got to stop that cow from wandering around."

"He's right about that at least," said the professor guy. "That cow ate my roses."

"I think I can solve all of this," said Harry. "That's Ed Hammerstein's cow, but it's his father's pasture. I'll go talk to Able and he'll do something about it, I'm sure of it."

The two city men chatted with each other for a moment and then the professor guy said, "We'd appreciate that."

"Fine," said Harry. "Now, how about an ice cream. On me. As an apology."

The two men made happy noises and Harry took them over to the freezer that Ed's cow had licked and scooped each of them a vanilla ice-cream cone. They left the store all smiles. When my mother brought her groceries up to the counter, Harry nodded out the window at Al and the professor guy eating their ice creams. "Just like them to come in and complain," said Harry. "Never seen them lift a finger to chase that cow back in." Harry looked back at my mother. "How about you, then? How does a free ice cream sound?"

"Well," said my mother.

"Sounds good, don't it?" said Harry.

Harry scooped up another couple of cones and gave them to us. My mom and I both knew the ice cream was a bribe to keep our mouths shut, but we left the store smiling all the same.

Harry drove his pickup over to talk to Able. No one knows what went on there, but it's a shameful thing when a neighbour has to complain to your face. If you've got a complaint about your neighbour in Likely, you go down to the Cafe and do a little talking there, and eventually word gets around. Able, of course, must have felt the shame of it all, and the shame fuelled anger. He started up the tractor and revved it down to Ed's shop. Uncle Horace was there at the time, picking up his beef, so of course we heard all about it.

Had Able been polite and said, "Ed, my son, that cow of yours is a bit of a problem. Maybe we can work together towards a solution that would keep her contained and not defecating on the streets of our fine town," then Ed might have kept the cow confined to another field, one not so close to Likely. But Able has never been a polite man, and he didn't use the word "defecate" and he didn't take into account Ed's feelings on the matter. He said, "You keep that goddamned cow locked up or so help me God I'll shoot her!"

Bjarne Lindskoog was one of the last people to see Ed's cow alive. She was munching on the lilac bush that grew in front of the house belonging to the professor guy. When Bjarne went to tell Ed about the cow, Ed was on the phone with his father, and Able was so angry Lindskoog could hear his voice. "You wouldn't do nothing about her, so I did," Able shouted. "I shot her just off Second Street near the tracks. You go pick her up quick and you got steak." Ed hung up, and after he'd dealt with Bjarne, he took his pickup over to see that his fence-crawling cow was there, just off Second Street, dead. Able had shot the cow between the eyes and then slit her throat to bleed, so she could still be butchered and used for meat. Able is nothing if not practical.

You never see a man cry in Likely. Crying is a private thing a man does while sitting on the toilet with his pants down in the bathroom when his crop fails. But Ed stood by the side of the road with his arms hanging limp beside him and sobbed beside that cow. Uncle George drove by, and Rudy too, and Mom and Dad and I heard about it when we met them at the Cafe. That day was a Saturday. We were supposed to be down at the church site constructing, but it had rained for fifteen minutes at eight o'clock that morning, so we were all down at the Cafe instead.

About half an hour later Ed went by the Cafe in his front end loader, carrying the body of that cow along Centre Avenue slow, like in a funeral procession, leaving a line of cow's blood down the middle of the street. We all stood up and followed Ed as he drove to the Texas house pasture. Mrs. Shute and Nevil came out of their backyard. Harry Wyton closed up the store and joined us. Wallace left his wife, Evangeline, in charge of the dealership and came out too. We all stood at the fence and watched as Ed dug a hole and buried the cow behind the Texas house a little ways off from the monkey's grave.

The next we heard Ed Hammerstein had slammed himself and Mrs. Shute's Duster into a power pole.

Ed's funeral was one of the few I can remember where the whole town shut down to go. We were all feeling a little guilty for our parts in the cow's death, and none of us had had the time to set things right with Ed, so to miss his funeral seemed a social sin of the worse kind. The Cafe closed, Harry locked the doors of the General Store, and Wallace Hammerstein closed the tractor dealership so that his entire family could attend his brother's funeral. Even Able took a full day off from field work to mourn his son. Able had only taken a half-day off for his wife Anna's funeral, but of course she'd gone and died smack in the middle of planting season.

The day my father told Nevil and me that Ed had died, Nevil was getting some practice driving the tractor and hay rack, and Dad and I were riding the back of the tractor giving him advice. Nevil drove the hay rack onto a side hill and the bales gave way and twenty or thirty of them fell off. Not much you can do to stop a thing like that, so we drove the rest of them home and unloaded them, then went back for the bales that had fallen off and stacked them back on the hay rack. When we were finished stacking Dad drove the tractor and hay rack home and Nevil and I collapsed on the field.

"Jesus, I'm soaked," said Nevil. "Weird thing, about Ed dying."

"Yeah," I said.

"You can die any time," he said. "You can be driving along the highway and bam!"

"Yeah," I said.

Nevil slugged me in the shoulder. It was the usual invitation to a wrestle, but I felt suddenly angry and pushed Nevil on his back and got him in a headlock and really tried to hurt him. I didn't. He pushed me off and pinned me down and then we rolled a little ways down the slope of the coulee. Nevil kneed me in the thigh hard enough that tears came to my eyes. I pushed him off and rolled away and sat up with my hands around my knees. Nevil grinned and threw himself on the slope of the coulee next to me. "You okay?" he said. "Did I hurt you?"

"Nope," I said.

We sat for a time looking over the swamp at the base of the coulee and the prairie beyond. Nevil used my shoulder to get up and then held out his hand. I didn't take it. I scrambled up by myself and dusted off my pants. It was a small thing, not accepting his hand up, but it marked the beginning of the end of our childhood friendship and we both knew it. Nevil walked a little farther away from me than usual as we went back to the house for coffee. I shoved my hands a little deeper into my pockets and pressed the place on my thigh where the bruise was growing.

GET ME A LOVE POTION

I SPENT most of my childhood believing the world would end before I reached puberty, so when puberty hit before the world ended, I wasn't prepared. There were no great love affairs going on in the community for me to watch and learn from, save the love blossoming before our eyes in the front pew of Lamentations Church between Abbie Slabie, Dorothy's older sister, a woman with the sweetness and logic of a five-year-old, and Squirrely Johnson, a man of normal intelligence who was, well, socially challenged. He played marbles in the dirt in front of the General Store with the eight-year-olds, and he played to win. My sister, Louise, and Russell Schmidt had eloped, of course, but I saw little romance in getting married on a whim, in your jeans, by a justice of the peace, and then going off to live in a cow pasture. Louise had denied us all a wedding and reception and she was resented for it. In Likely sanctioned parties are hard to come by.

There were Miss Gray and Mr. Dyck, who were well into their sixties and who never married each other or anyone else — they were both so shy they didn't own phones — but they'd been singing sweetly to each other in the Lamentations Church choir lo these many years. The only romance with any drama was the one in which Rudy Bierlie, the shop instructor, made a fool of himself over Mrs. Noyes, the elementary teacher, who responded in kind when she was a blonde but not when she was brunette. But that ended when Mrs. Noyes took a year-long sabbatical to get some therapy and came back with a set of contacts, a single personality, and only one wig (the blonde was gone).

In most small communities the best place to find a little romance is the Saturday dance, and folks did put on dances in the area, just not the folks from Lamentations Church or the Hereford Club or the 4-H club. Dancing was the first sin, card-playing the second, then it went on to adultery, mouthing off to one's parents, cattle-rustling, telling falsehoods and murder. My cousin Sharon, Uncle Horace and Aunt Marion's daughter, was musical; she could play any instrument she got her hands on. When Sharon was a little girl, Aunt Marion, who was raised a Lutheran, said, "Sharon's going to be a dancer; you can feel it in her, the way she moves to music."

"No kid of mine's going to be a dancer," said Uncle Horace. But if you did the math you'd know Sharon was born just five months after Horace and Marion were married.

Susan danced. From the moment in grade 6 math when I discovered the funny way the hair on her neck extended almost to her shoulder line, I adored Susan. In my dreams I saw us in front of fireplaces, in my father's pickup, in the coulee back of our place, under the bleachers at the baseball diamond. Always, even as I sat out the final days of class in my graduating year, all we did in my fantasies was hold hands. "Martin," she would say. "Oh, Martin." I couldn't imagine what else she would say; I'd hardly ever talked to her. I didn't know how. In the final months of my graduating year, I began to see this as a real problem.

There were only two people in Likely I trusted enough to take my problems to. Sometimes I went to Pastor Gottlieb, but if I was too afraid to talk to him, I went to Mrs. Shute. When Nevil and I were still close friends, I had visited Mrs. Shute's house almost every day. I knew her well enough to stop in unannounced, and even after Nevil and I grew apart, I often dropped by. Her house was cluttered with all kinds of stuff, like the old cream separator in the living room, and canning jars filled with polished stones on the bookshelves, and, in summer, zucchinis on the couch, potatoes on the floor, beets in the bathroom sink. I liked Mrs. Shute. She gave me large bowls of ice cream. I could talk to her.

"There's this girl," I said.

"Ah, and you like her," said Mrs. Shute.

I nodded. "How do you go about — " I said, and made a hand gesture she could interpret in a number of ways.

"How do you go about asking a girl out?" she said.

I shrugged.

"How do you go about making a pass?" she said.

I shrugged again.

"Or is it, how do you go about all of it?"

I looked at my thumbnail and nodded. Mrs. Shute patted my hand. "Don't worry," she said. "Lots of men, plenty older than you, don't know which end is up." That didn't help and I told her so.

"You and this girl," said Mrs. Shute, "you get together, and nature will take over, you'll see." I didn't understand but I didn't tell her that. I went home and reread the instruction pamphlet inside my mother's tampon box.

It was during my eighteenth year, the year my Uncle George moved to Edmonton and rented me his farm, that the thought occurred to me: I must be one of the 144,000 chosen — the ones "who did not defile themselves with women," the ones chosen by God who "follow the lamb wherever he goes." Then I thought, no, I couldn't be one of the chosen, I was given to self-abuse; I must then be the anti-Christ. Despite my Christian rearing, this held a certain fascination. Then I thought — in a burst of fundamentalist literalism — maybe the temptation of lust was not beyond the chosen: why exactly did the 144,000 chosen follow sheep around?

What got me on this train of thought was the twelve-hundred-pound bull savagely breeding my heifer calf. The bull belonged to my father, and had just bred my heifer four times in the last three minutes. I was standing on the outside of the fence on my Uncle George's property that enclosed this lovemaking, with the top of the fence under my armpits. It was a perilous position. I could be kicked, horned or pinned at any moment. But then I was young and despondent. My life stretched out before me, empty of my one desire: woman.

I credit this moment of contemplation as a turning point. It was here, standing on the fence, watching procreation in all its glory — the bull rising like a red-faced drunk, his penis pumped, primed and leaking, his hoofs bruising the heifer's hip bones for that three seconds of intercourse — that I realized the height my frustration had reached. I had gone the traditional route in search of a mate — the Lamentations Church suppers, senior 4-H events, the livestock auction coffee shop, prayers to the Almighty — and it had failed me. I was virginal at a time when John Travolta bought his condoms in bulk.

Desperate times warrant desperate measures. I went to see Pastor Gottlieb, who was, like everyone else in Likely, a cattleman. "Um, I want to talk about marriage," I said.

He was surprised. "Marriage?" he said. "Who's the lucky girl?"

"No, no," I said. "I'm not marrying anybody, at least not yet."

"Ah," he said. "Then, what?"

"I want to be ... prepared."

"Prepared?" said Gottlieb. "Ah, prepared." His eyes narrowed. "You're not thinking of being ... prepared before you're lawfully united in marriage," he said.

"No, no," I said.

"The Lord spreads the evil of disease on those disposed to be ... prepared before their union is sanctified by the Lord."

"No. I mean yes," I said.

"He prevents unlawful union before it takes place. He turns the rod to a snake at the very moment of crisis, if you get my meaning."

Gottlieb's voice softened. "Of course the marital union of a man and woman is God's destiny fulfilled," he said. "Like the bull and his cow, a man and a woman who do not complete the marital act are committing a sin against the great producer, the great farmer of us all. We're here to produce God's children."

I nodded; I didn't know what else to do. He patted my hand. "You're a good boy," he said. "Your daddy raised you good. Read this."

Pastor Gottlieb handed me *The Loving Art of Marriage*. Mysteries were revealed. From the book I learned 1 per cent of the Christian population in the United States in 1956 thought oral sex was okay; I learned a husband should never pester his wife for lovemaking when she has the Curse; and I learned how to wash and reroll condoms for economy's sake.

There wasn't, however, a section on kissing. I'd never kissed or been kissed by anybody. The book did not explain what oral sex was, and it said, "Don't worry about the size of your penis; everyone inflates to the same size." Baloney. My father's bull could scratch his brisket with his penis.

I went to visit Mrs. Shute again and told her I was worried. "You've got one, right?" she said. I nodded. "Then there's nothing to worry about."

"Doesn't it matter," I said, "how long?"

"I never met a woman yet who gave a hoot," said Mrs. Shute. "Rough hands, now that's a problem."

I made a mental note to grease my hands with udder balm.

"And the kissing," I said. "I never kissed anybody."

"Sometimes you get a bull," she said, "a young one, and you put him into the herd and he just stands there. He's never been with cows before, you understand. He's not doing his job. What do you do?"

"Dad and I just leave him in there," I said. "With the herd. Usually one of the cows in heat jumps on top of him, kind of shows him how to do it, until he gets the idea."

"So these old cows show the young bull how to do it? And don't even the young cows sometimes know better than the bull what to do?"

"Yeah, heifers are always jumping each other. Put an untried bull in with them and they'll jump him. He gets the idea pretty quick."

"Yes," said Mrs. Shute. "Now you get the idea?"

I went home and thought about it. It was during this time of contemplation that I decided to ask Susan to the fire-hall dance. This was risky, not only because Susan could very easily say no, but because heaven only knows what would happen if my mother heard I'd been there.

"Susan," I said. "You going to the dance at the fire-hall Saturday?"

"Yeah," she said. "You going?"

"Yeah," I said.

"Great," she said. "You got a date?"

"No," I said. "Want to go with me?"

"Yeah, great," she said.

That was how it was supposed to go.

"Hi, Susan," I said. "You going to the dance at the fire-hall Saturday?"

"What?" she said.

"I was wondering if you were going to the dance Saturday."

"Oh. Yeah," she said and looked down the street. We were just outside the General Store. "I always go," said Susan.

"Me too," I said.

"You?" she said. "I've never seen you there. Your mom would skin you."

"I've been there," I said. "Lots of times."

"What was that?" said Susan.

"You want to go to the dance with me?" I said, too loud, so that Mrs. Mulder, who was coming out of the store, looked at me. Susan laughed. She laughed. I can still see the filling at the back of her mouth.

"What are we going to do?" she said. "Hold hands in the corner while everybody else dances?" That was in fact what I'd envisaged. "You're a little boy," said Susan.

That really happened. All I've told you is God's truth, of course, but that is the worst story I've got from my young years. I was crushed. I couldn't stand Likely any longer. There was the baseball diamond where she hadn't held my hand, the pickup we hadn't sat in, the store where she'd dumped me.

I paid Mrs. Shute another visit. "So it was Susan, was it?" said Mrs. Shute.

I nodded and drank the last of the coffee in my cup. Mrs. Shute refilled it. "Sometimes what we want isn't so good for us," said Mrs. Shute.

"I know, I know," I said.

"There'll be another girl," said Mrs. Shute. "But of course you know that too."

I nodded miserably, though I knew I was one of those fools who wasn't destined to find love.

"You tell me," said Mrs. Shute. "What is it you like about Susan? What is it you want in a girl?"

I'd never stopped to think about why I liked Susan, except for her hairline. What did I want in a girl?

"I'd like a pretty girl," I said.

"You and all the other men who watch television," said Mrs. Shute. She poured herself more coffee, rolled a pumpkin off a chair and sat. "You want a pretty girl," she said.

"Yes."

"Blonde hair?"

"Yes," I said eagerly. "And blue eyes. Hair down to here. Not too much make-up. Dutch or German is okay. But not Norwegian. She'd have to know how to make squares. But then Mom can give her some recipes. I'm not picky."

"Not Norwegian," said Mrs. Shute.

I fidgeted with my cup. Mrs. Shute poured us both some more coffee. We drank. "Sometimes," said Mrs. Shute, "we don't get what we want because we want it too much."

"Couldn't you just give me something?" I said.

"Something like what?"

"You know, something to get women to like me?"

"A love potion?"

I knew these things existed because Pastor Gottlieb

preached against their kind in church about twice a year. "There are Foreign Influences among us!" he'd say, and sweat. "Evil Influences that will tell you lies, offer you false cures, muddle your mind with liquor. Foreign Influences that promise unholy health and happiness from pills and potions that are sanctioned neither by God nor Western Medicine!"

Everybody knew who the Foreign Influence was. There was only one Foreign Influence in Likely: Mrs. Shute.

"Listen," said Mrs. Shute. "If I had this magic potion, do you think I'd live alone, here, in Likely?"

I hadn't considered that. "I heard you make ... preparations," I said.

"Who told you this?"

"Everybody knows. Even Pastor Gottlieb says."

"Gottlieb," said Mrs. Shute. "Listen, I'll tell you a story about Gottlieb. Some time ago he comes in here looking for carrots because he says his wife doesn't have any. Then, when he sees no one else is around, he says, I'm having trouble, you know, getting it up. He says, My wife is complaining, can you do anything for it? The mischief gets into me and I say, Okay, drink this, and I hand him a bottle of my strawberry cordial. Then I say, Spit three times. And he does. Then I wrap that glass ball, the one I used to keep on the fireplace, in a dishrag. Put this in your pants, I say. And he does. Now, I say, we'll inspect the offending organ. He says, Is that necessary? I say, Yes. So into his pants I go, and what do you know, he grows! Just look, I say, at the rabbit I scared up for the fox."

"So it worked," I said. "You helped him."

"He hasn't been back."

"I want to find a girl. A pretty girl. Settle down. I want love."

"Maybe you should think about something else for a while," she said. "Get a hobby. Go fishing. Get out of Likely for a while. Why not go to college?"

"I suppose," I said.

"When love comes," said Mrs. Shute, "it will take you by surprise."

I was three years into my agriculture program when I finally met a woman, the woman I would eventually marry. She was in the supper line ahead of me at the student union cafeteria, wearing a blue dress with some lace along the neckline, sleeves and hem that gave her a distinctly elderly air. She wore runners and a beer cap. She was trying to match her cutlery. "I don't believe this," she said, and rummaged.

"You were at that competition," I said. "The weed identification competition."

"Yeah, yeah," she said and clanked spoons.

"You got lady's thumb and green smartweed, three seconds flat," I said. "I'd never tell them apart."

Somebody yelled, "Get a move on, lady." She raised her head from the cutlery and held up a fork. "Stick it," she yelled back at the line.

"You were amazing," I said.

She looked at me as if she'd just noticed me, and smiled. For that split second she was pretty. The smile faded. "You should've got the rough cinquefoil and henbane," she said. "Easy."

She picked out her cutlery and we shuffled down the food line. "I'm not good with weeds," I said. "I'm better with anatomy." That would've been a line if I knew what a line was. "Martin Winkle," I said. "From Likely."

She shook my hand. "Lena Henkleman," she said. "From Vulcan."

"Lena," I said.

"This place stinks," she said. "They don't even have saucers for the cups."

"Yeah," I said. "I know what you mean."

"You into going over to High Level?" she said.

High Level Diner was three blocks down near the bridge over the North Saskatchewan River, where each February at reading break at least one student jumped to his or her death upon the frozen river. The restaurant had a wonderful view.

"You mean leave this?" I said. I had the tiny beef dip with limp bread and cold brown stuff in a bowl.

"Yeah, I hate eating alone."

This was a revelation to me. Not only was a girl asking me out, and I was accepting, but we were leaving a restaurant without eating or paying for our food. We left our trays on the counter where we'd stood. Talk about breaking the rules. Talk about rebellion.

We discussed weeds until we found seats at the diner. "What are you getting?" said Lena, and she fixed me with a long look over her menu. "I'm going for the steak sandwich. I like red meat."

If I'd known better I would've recognized that as flirtation.

"Oh, the toasted tomato," I said.

Over dinner we talked about our families, our friends back home, the towns we'd grown up in. Lena's home town of Vulcan — the little town that would one day wear Spock ears to save itself from economic extinction — was a town very much like Likely. We talked about the games we'd played. "Crokinole!" said Lena. "I love crokinole. You got a board?"

"Sure," I said. "You could come over and play."

It didn't occur to me until I put the key into the lock of

my apartment and held open the door for Lena that I had asked a woman over to my place. The implications were overwhelming. "You're a slob," said Lena. "You set up the crokinole board and I'll tidy up."

She picked a few socks off the carpet and tilted her head at me. "You have matching dishes?" she said. I nodded. "Cutlery?"

"A set my mother gave me," I said.

"Good," she said and spent half an hour picking up socks, underwear, shirts and filthy dishes and piling them all in my closet. I set up the crokinole board. The point of crokinole is to shoot the other guy's checkers off the board and get your own checker into the hole. It's trickier than it sounds. There are pegs on the board that stop your checker from skidding across. It's all very strategic. Lena lost her balance in a tricky move, fell over the crokinole board and accidentally stuck her tongue in my mouth. "Oh, I'm sorry," she said when she saw the look on my face. After a pause she said, "I thought you were interested. I mean, inviting me over for crokinole and all."

"No," I said. "I mean I am. Interested."

"You looked so shocked."

"It's just, well, I never."

She coloured. "Never?" she said.

I bowed my head.

She looked me over as if she were examining a new weed. "Well," she said. "We'll fix that."

During moments like this, the awesome implications of decision-making overwhelm me. If I hadn't talked to Mrs. Shute that day I might have decided to stay on my father's farm in Likely, and if I hadn't decided to go away to school, I wouldn't have gone to the cafeteria that day. If I hadn't gone to the cafeteria, Lena wouldn't have flattened me over the crokinole board, or put her hot hands through the hole in my Jockey shorts, nor would she have done something painful and thrilling to my neck. I hadn't wished for these things. I'd wished for a pretty blonde girl with good teeth, not a weed specialist; I'd dreamed of holding hands and embracing under the stars, not panting and tumbling over the crokinole checkers. But then, if Lena baked squares, I'd have long since gone to fat. Mrs. Shute said it best that day of the love potion. "There's an old pagan curse," she said. "May all your prayers be answered, and may you always get what you wish for."

TREATISE ON MIRACLES

THE problem was this: my love, Lena, was an agnostic feminist weed specialist who had just converted to vegetarianism. My parents had not gone farther afield than Ponoka in forty years and my father's idea of a good time was going out after church to shoot gophers. My mother, despite her actions to the contrary, firmly believed the wife should submit to her husband, just as the husband submits to God. I think you can understand me when I say I was squeamish about Lena and my parents meeting up. That's why they hadn't, even though Lena and I had been seeing each other for almost a year. More importantly, I did not want my parents to know Lena and I were more or less living together. This is what Lena and I were arguing about, again, in my little basement apartment in Edmonton.

"I don't believe it," said Lena. "Did you time-warp here from the fifties or something?"

It's sometimes two days and two sleepless nights before I can come up with a really good snarky remark, so I didn't say anything. I turned my back on Lena and strode into the kitchen (well, I didn't really stride — it was only two steps from the bed to the fridge) and made myself a sandwich. Don't get me wrong. Lena was everything I'd been looking for. She was female, bright, rebellious, and she had sex with me. When I walked with Lena through the crowded corridors of the University of Alberta, a banty rooster could not have walked as proudly. I wanted to live with her. But I was also afraid. I was afraid my mother would call my place in the middle of the night on some emergency and I wouldn't be there and she'd panic and call the police, or worse, she'd suspect I was staying overnight at Lena's. There was also the threat that my mother would find out Lena was living with me. But my parents don't leave Likely, unless absolutely necessary, so the only way my mother would figure out Lena was living with me was if Lena answered the phone a lot during odd hours — after 9:00 P.M. or before eight in the morning. I didn't have the guts to tell Lena she couldn't answer the phone — that would only increase the likelihood that she would — so I ran for it each time it rang and cried, "I'll get it!" I lived in constant fear. This was the time before widespread use of answering machines, God's gift to people like me.

I didn't get a lot of phone calls. But I did get one this night, and that's what had started the argument all over again. Lena was sitting right next to the phone when it rang and my fingers were covered in biscuit batter. She reached for the phone but I panicked and pulled the phone off the table by its cord, slid across the linoleum in my stocking feet and grabbed the receiver off the floor with my dough-covered fingers, Rambo-style. "Hello?" I said.

This may all seem strange, being so afraid of my parents finding out I was living with Lena, but that fear was by no means uncommon in the student body of the agricultural department of the U of A. There were young couples, gay and straight — our future farmers and agricultural experts — frantically sneaking around, lying secretly with each other in the biblical sense, then lying poorly but successfully to their parents, who wanted to believe they'd raised moral children and turned a blind eye to evidence that they had not.

What was different in our case was that Lena had given her parents my phone number — they weren't church-going people and they were already growing soybeans — and she resented the fact that I wouldn't tell my own folks. Our present living arrangement was impractical; we were spending a lot of money on a second apartment we didn't need. Lena thought I was being childish, and to make matters worse, I acted in distinctly childish ways. I still went home weekends and holidays to work for my father — that was how I financed my education, and Lena didn't fault me for that. What she did fault me for was taking home my laundry for my mother to do, and my mending. I wasn't alone here either. Most young males in the agricultural program were taking their laundry home for their mothers to do on weekends, and bringing back meals prepared by their mothers to get them through the week. I made my own meals, and most of Lena's, something I was proud of here, in Edmonton, but somewhat ashamed of in Likely.

"You don't want anyone to know I'm here," said Lena.

I couldn't deny it and I couldn't justify it, so I took my sandwich into the bathroom to eat in privacy. Lena yelled through the door, competing with the television that I'd left on. "When are you going to grow up?" said Lena. "You can't go on sneaking around, kowtowing to these archaic rules you don't agree with."

Lena was wrong there. I knew I could kowtow forever. Everyone in my hometown of Likely did just that. But I said nothing. Lena hadn't met my parents yet, so there was no way she could really understand. We were having this argument again because that had been my sister, Louise, on the phone. Louise was coming up to Edmonton to stay with me for a day or two to do some job hunting. Several months before she had finally left Russell and was now living in a small apartment in Camrose. She would arrive that evening, and I was trying to explain to Lena why I didn't want Lena to stay the night.

"But I want to meet Louise," said Lena through the bathroom door.

"I want you to meet her," I said. "I just don't want you to stay the night. It doesn't look good."

"You're ashamed of me!"

"No!" I said. "It just doesn't look good."

"How're you going to explain my clothes in the closet and my stuff in the bathroom?"

I opened the door to the bathroom and came out with Lena's stuff in a plastic bag. "I thought you could take it with you."

"You're kicking me out!" said Lena.

I went over to the television set, and as a courtesy, I turned off the sound, and then got caught in the hypnotic image of three small men jumping into a bowl of cereal. "No, I'm not," I said. "I love you. I want you here. Just not tonight."

"I've got a better idea," said Lena. "Louise can stay at my place. I'll stay here with you." I gave her a pleading look. "All right, I'll stay at my place and Louise can also stay at my place. I've got more room."

I'd thought of this, but that would give Lena and Louise time alone together to exchange notes. "I think she'd feel more comfortable staying here," I said. "She's bringing an air mattress. Look, I just don't want Louise to know we're living together. That's all it's about."

"She's your sister, not your mother," said Lena.

In fact, Louise was getting to be more like my mother every time I saw her, which wasn't often. She'd been working as a manager for Ned's Pancake House in Camrose and so she was no longer wearing jeans and T-shirts; instead she wore white button earrings and white plastic bead necklaces that, from a distance, looked like pearls. Like my mother, Louise was punctual, dependable and reliable, and her nails were chewed to the quick.

"I don't see what you're worried about," said Lena.

"It'll get back to Mom and Dad," I said.

"If we ask her not to, she won't tell them."

"Oh, yes she will," I said.

"Isn't this just like you meat-eaters," said Lena. "You go out with the boys to shoot defenceless gophers like big apes, but you're too afraid to stand up to your own family."

I've found, in my life with Lena, that once arguments begin degenerating into mud-flinging, they're pretty much over. Once it gets this ridiculous, you've got to fight back the giggles in order to stay angry. Inspiration struck me. "Vegetarian farts are the worst," I said. "All those beans."

Now there, there was the crucial point. It was either laugh or go into a rage. Lena chose to rage. She marched around the apartment collecting her clothes, shoes and "family planning" items in order to once again leave me. She picked up the tube of spermicide and pointed it at me. "You are a wimp," she said. "You're so scared you can't see straight. You're so afraid to be seen doing anything 'sinful' that you'll lie to avoid it. It's all show, no substance. Why can't you stand up for something for once?"

I shrugged. Lena pitched the tube of spermicide at me, threw her clothes on the floor and slammed out the door. I sat on the couch and waited. I knew what would happen next. Lena would wait in the hall until I came out to urge her back into the apartment (or until the apartment manager came down to the utility room just off my apartment, which had happened twice, the only two times Lena came to me first). She'd sit on the couch looking angry until I said I was sorry for the remark about the vegetarian farts, and then she would admit to some excessive hostility over the gopher-shooting issue. Then I'd say, No, you're right. I am a wimp. But could you please stay at your place for a couple of nights until Louise's visit is over? And she'd say, Yes, I'll live this sham for you; if it means this much to you, I'll set aside my need for honesty and lie for you.

I knew this resolution would happen. The only problem was that my sister, Louise, turned up before it could take place. She knocked on my door. When I opened it Lena was standing beside her. "Oh!" I said.

"I was just on my way over from my apartment that I don't share with you," said Lena. "Louise and I met in the hallway. I knew it must be her. Louise has the same Winkle eyes."

Louise and I shook hands and I slapped her on the shoulder. "Good to see you," I said.

"That's it?" said Lena.

"What," I said.

"No hug?"

"Well," I said.

"Go on," said Lena, and so my sister, Louise, and I hugged each other, awkwardly, for the first time in our lives.

"Come in, come in," I said, then remembered Lena's clothes and effects scattered all over the floor, and stood my place in front of the door.

"Move," said Louise.

"Ah," I said.

"I was coming by to finish sorting the laundry," said Lena.

"I see that," said Louise.

"Sorry about the mess," I said. "Just give me a minute."

Lena squeezed in ahead of Louise, slipped the spermicide tube into her pocket and kicked the basket of condoms and K-Y jelly under the sofa-bed. I gathered her panties and undershirts, skirts and socks and threw them into the closet. "I thought Martin and I could do laundry together and save your mother some work," said Lena.

"You're still taking your laundry home?" said Louise.

"Well," I said.

"And his mending," said Lena.

"And Mom still puts up with that?" said Louise.

"I understand she's not too happy about it," said Lena. "But I don't know for sure, seeing as how I've never met your parents."

"You've never introduced Lena to Mom and Dad?" said Louise.

"Well," I said.

"I thought it was just me," said Louise. "Since it's so far to Camrose."

"We've been busy," I said.

"Yes, busy," said Lena, and she elbowed me. I looked down. I'd inadvertently nudged the basket of condoms out from under the sofa-bed with my heel. I nudged them back again.

"Well, I hope to see a lot more of you," said Louise, and she grinned. "Now that you're living together."

"Ah, Louise," I said. "We're not living together."

"Yeah, sure," said Louise.

"I still have my apartment," said Lena.

"Martin, God did not give you the ability to lie," said

Louise. "Your left ear goes red and you get a tic under your eye. There it is there. You also get spots on your neck."

I touched my neck. "Spots?" I said.

"And he gets sweaty," said Lena. "Across his forehead."

"I'm not lying!" I said.

"There's the tic," said Louise.

"He gets that before exams too," said Lena.

"I mean, I don't want Mom and Dad to think that," I said. "About us living together. I don't want them to get the wrong idea."

"They won't get any ideas from me," said Louise.

I made tea and brought out the plastic tub of squares Mom had sent down with me the weekend before. I put them on the coffee table in front of the TV. I'd decided to leave the television on, with the sound turned off, because it was one of only three light sources in my apartment. Lena made a point of not helping me. We talked of this and that, and then Louise brought up the improbable subject of miracles.

"Last Wednesday the last of my cheque ran out," said Louise. "And I was out of hand soap, and when I went to get the mail, there was a package there from an old school friend of mine — remember Shirley Clapstein? And you know what it was? It was a little box of gift soap. God works in miraculous ways."

"That's not a miracle," said Lena. "That's synchronicity."

"Well, whatever it was, I appreciated it," said Louise.

"Martin, tell her about the money," said Lena.

"Nah," I said.

"Money, what money?" said Louise.

"Martin keeps finding five dollars, the same five dollars, and he keeps spending it, and it keeps turning up."

"How do you know it's the same five dollars?" said Louise.

"It has this weird inscription on it," said Lena. "How does it go?"

" 'There is no reason in the roasting of eggs,' " I said.

"But he finds it everywhere," said Lena. "Always when he's broke."

"I found it in a book once, in the library," I said. "I reached for the book off the shelf, opened it, and the five dollars fell out."

"Somebody's playing a trick on you," said Louise. "Or somebody's written that on all kinds of bills."

"I thought that too, at first," I said. "So I marked the five dollars with a little doodle in the corner. Then I found it again, this time in the cubicle in the washroom."

"Nobody could play a trick that elaborate," said Lena. "Whoever it was would have to have half the city collaborating. He's got that same five dollars back as change in three different supermarkets."

"Well," said Louise.

Lena looked at me. "Should we tell her about the other thing?" she said.

"What other thing?" said Louise.

I told the story of how I'd come home from a date with Lena one morning in a dreamy euphoria, and gone to hang up my coat on the coat hook behind the door. I missed, but instead of falling to the floor, the coat had hung suspended on a beam of sunlight that came through the adjacent window. I'd stood watching it with delight and surprise until morning moved the sunlight past my window, and the coat fell.

Louise doubted the truth of my miracles, godless as they were. "That's impossible," she said. I must have been hung over and imagined the episode with the coat, she said, and it couldn't be the same five-dollar bill I found each time I ran out of money either. But when I produced it, the bill with the cryptic message scrawled in black ink, she looked uncertain. "So, let's say these things did happen," she said. "What's the reason behind them? There has to be some reason."

"How am I supposed to know why this stuff happens?" I said.

"It's that ball," said Lena. She went to the kitchen cupboard and took down the glass ball that had once sat on Mrs. Shute's fireplace mantel. I kept it in an egg cup on the top shelf.

"That's Mrs. Shute's ball," said Louise.

"It's my ball now," I said.

"A thing like that can't belong to anyone," said Lena. She held it up and looked at us through it, dramatically. I could see her face in the ball, upside-down.

Before I met Lena, the last I'd seen of the ball was when Nevil Shute threw it away over the coulee into Bjarne Lindskoog's field. The ball was a scratched-up old thing. I hadn't seen anything special about it, except the stories that everyone told. I had passed those stories on to Lena when we first started dating, in an attempt to be entertaining, and of course she lamented the ball had been lost to a cow pasture. So the next weekend when I went home to work at Dad's farm, in an uncharacteristic flow of romantic gesture, I'd decided to go hunting in Bjarne Lindskoog's field for the small glass ball that had, by that time, probably been ploughed under, ploughed up, eaten by cows, shit out, trampled on, burrowed by gophers and ploughed up again.

The day was Sunday, and I knew Bjarne Lindskoog would be home from church and inside the house finishing up his lunch. Lindskoog was one of my favourite people in Likely. He was well into his sixties at the time, but still milking a respectable herd of forty cows. When I came up to the house, Bjarne's wife Golda was just heading for her car. "Go right in," she said. "Bjarne's in the kitchen." He was, all right, sitting at the kitchen table, drinking coffee and looking over the *Western Producer*. He stood up, grinned, shook my hand and slapped me on the shoulder. I find in Lindskoog a kindred spirit. He's a storyteller but poor at lying. You know he's telling you a good one when he starts to scratch under his armpit. The bigger the bullshit, the harder the scratch.

"Martin," he said. "Haven't seen you around for a long time. What's up?"

I got down to business pretty quick. Bjarne said, "Sure I seen that ball." It had turned up as he was ploughing the year before, and he'd put it on a fence post to collect it later. Then he more or less forgot about it. We took his pickup and a couple of .22s and went out into the field. Not much use going into a field that time of year without popping off a few gophers. As I grew up, shooting gophers had been my favourite recreation, especially on Sundays, but after living part time in the city for several years and experiencing Lena's influence, the sport seemed, well, bloodthirsty. Once my father shot a gopher and the bullet tore the thing open so its belly slid out, and we watched through our sights as the animal stood on its hind legs and pawed at its guts trying to put them back in. That time I laughed and laughed — gophers were our enemies and the frantic gesture seemed comic. This time, as I shot a gopher and heard that characteristic "plop" as the shell ripped through its belly and it scrambled down its hole to go through its death throes in private, I began to understand Lena's objections.

"Why you want that ball anyways," said Lindskoog.

"Lena, my girlfriend, wants to see it," I said. "I told her about it."

"Well, let's go find it," he said. It didn't take long at all.

The ball was still perched in a rough hollow in the fence post, plastered with bird shit that acted as a kind of glue. I pried the ball off, dunked it in a puddle and rubbed off most of the shit with my shirttails. I held the ball up and looked around through it. Nothing much to see except the landscape upside-down.

"I never saw nothing in it," I said. "I don't know what everyone's on about."

"Yah, just stories," said Lindskoog. He took the ball from me and looked into it himself. "Although this thing must act like some kind of binoculars. That's the heifer I was going to get you to look at. She's not doing so good."

I took the ball back again and looked through it in the direction of Lindskoog's barns. Sure enough, there was a cow's head in there; it was that oddball of Lindskoog's, the one with the black face and the white ears and the seven on her forehead. She was chewing her cud. "Hmm," I said.

I turned and looked off over the field, in the direction of the gopher I'd just shot. I saw it, too, but it was in its hole, bloody and dead. I lowered the ball and rubbed my eyes. "Hell of a thing," I said. "You mind if I take it to show Lena?"

"No, no, you go right ahead," he said. "Keep it." I put the ball in my pocket and we got in the pickup and headed back to the barn. Lindskoog parked right in front and we went over to the heifer pens to take a look at the oddball.

"I cut down on her feed thinking she was getting a fat udder," said Lindskoog. "But it just kept getting bigger." I nodded. You don't want to overfeed a heifer; she won't milk so well later on if you do. This heifer's bag was big, like an older heifer's would be if she were about to calve.

"And this too," said Lindskoog. He held up her tail, and the heifer stepped from side to side and looked around at us.

Her vulva was growing off, expanding. It's usually a sure sign the cow's pregnant.

"You say she's not pregnant?" I said.

"None of these heifers is bred," said Lindskoog. "And I know no bull's come for a visit."

"You sure?" I said.

"They've been inside all the time," said Lindskoog. "I've had no break-ins."

"She sure looks pregnant," I said.

"Yah, sure she does," said Lindskoog.

"You checked?" I said.

"Didn't think it was possible," said Lindskoog. "Thought for sure she was sick. She's only seventeen months. There's been no bull near her."

"You got a glove, I'll check her," I said. Lindskoog brought me a plastic disposable glove that fitted to the shoulder. I pulled some of the manure from her rectum and ran my hand up there to check for pregnancy. You can feel the cow's uterus through the skin of her rectum. What I felt were two feet and a nose. She was about to calve. "Better get the chains," I said.

"So you're joking, eh?" said Lindskoog.

"Nope."

I pulled off the glove and, as Lindskoog went for the birthing chains, I put my arm up the heifer's vagina, found the calf's legs and pulled, hoping to ease its way a little. Never expect an easy birth on a heifer, especially one this young. The births are long, drawn-out events that go on for hours, and a good farmer will let the heifer push unassisted, only putting chains on the calf's legs to pull if the heifer is tiring or if there's a problem. The chains were a precaution; get them handy in case of a problem. But this heifer was an oddball in more ways than just the look of her. I pulled on the calf's legs and fell backwards. The calf slid from the heifer, like shit flows from a cow on grass, and landed partly on me, partly in the straw. I pulled mucus from the calf's nose and the heifer was on me and that calf immediately. A lot of heifers take a few births before they get the hang of mothering, of licking off the calf to get its lungs and circulation going. Not this one. She was licking the calf and eyeing me like I should get out of there quick. I did. The other heifers in the pen started dancing around, excited by the smell of the birthing. One of them came up and licked the calf, and the mother heifer banged her off.

Lindskoog carried the chains up to the pen as I was getting out of it. "You're joking," he said.

"Just like that," I said. "She hardly pushed."

We stood there for quite a while, Lindskoog and me, and watched the heifer lick every inch of her calf. Within an hour the calf was standing on wobbly legs and sniffing around for his mother's black teats. There were two things we saw almost immediately: he was a bull calf, and he was the spitting image of his mother. For the calf to have every mark the same as his mother, well, that seemed to bear up the notion that this heifer was a virgin. You never get two cows with the same markings, ever, even with twins. But if this was God's chosen bull, he wasn't going to win any prizes at the Likely Fair. He was the kind of bull you get razzed about by neighbours. ("What'd you do, dip his ears in peroxide?")

The question was, as the product of a solid Christian rearing, what do you do with a bull calf born of a virgin? In Lindskoog's case, what you do is take a photograph of him next to his mother, put him in a calf pen that measures four by six feet, feed him milk replacer, and sell him as a vealer at Ponoka auction. Another messiah sacrificed for the good of humankind, or at least of the family from Camrose named Orton who bought him, butchered him and put him in their freezer. I told Louise all about it for the first time that night she met Lena in my apartment.

"That's impossible," said Louise. I shrugged and put on the saucepan I used to boil water to make another pot of tea. She took the ball from Lena and looked into it. "Well, nothing in there now," she said.

Lena shoved over beside Louise to look inside the ball with her, and I looked into it over my sister's shoulder. All I could see was the room upside-down. Then I looked down at Lena and realized something was terribly wrong. It was just a feeling at first, alarm bells going off in the back of my head. Then I realized what it was. The picture on the television set was still; not just focussed on one image, but totally still. I could see each individual dot, and light was streaking from the screen.

"What's going on?" said Lena. I looked at the clock. Its hands were still. I walked over to the pot of boiling water and called my sister and Lena. We stared into the pot in awe. The bubbling of the hot water was still, as if caught in a photograph. Steam hung suspended in the air above the pot.

"Oh, my God," said Louise.

"Outside!" said Lena.

We ran down the hallway and outside onto the lawn in front of the apartment building. Everything was still: cars in traffic, people caught in their steps. Car exhaust hung strangely motionless. A seagull floated in the air low above us, as if hung on strings; its shit was suspended in the space above our heads. More spooky than any of this was the quiet, complete quiet, like nothing I've ever heard.

"It's the ball," said Lena. Louise held the ball up. We all

looked at it and suddenly the world was noisy again. Cars moved, pedestrians ran, the bird shit hit the side of my head.

We walked, stunned, back into my little apartment and closed the door. Louise put the ball on the coffee table and sat down on the couch next to Lena. I washed bird dooey from my hair in the bathroom sink.

"It's a miracle," said Lena.

"That wasn't a miracle," said Louise.

"Why not?" said Lena.

"A miracle has to make sense, it's got to be for some reason," said Louise. "Otherwise it's just a hallucination or something."

"Why does it have to have a reason?" said Lena.

"It just does," said Louise. "Otherwise it doesn't come from God."

"Well, maybe there is a reason and we don't know it," I said.

"Do all miracles have to come from some God?" said Lena. "Maybe miracles are just the way of things."

"It must be a sign of the end times," said Louise.

"Oh, come on," said Lena.

"How about some soybean burgers?" I said. Louise made a face and Lena ignored me. "Tea?" I said.

"Oh, I don't know," said Lena. "Maybe it *is* the end of the world. How do you explain something like that?"

Ironic, isn't it? When I had grappled and prayed for miracles as an adolescent ("Whatever a man prays for, he prays for a miracle," Pastor Gottlieb had taught us), I hadn't found them. It was only when I apparently turned my back on faith, fell in love with Lena and left the desperate search behind me that miracles fell into my lap. I don't know why time stopped for those few minutes, just as I don't know why the virgin cow gave birth or why I still find that five dollars.

There was no more rhyme or reason to this miracle than to any of the others. I've searched for connections — the ball was the door to it all, certainly, but why did the three of us bear witness? Was that blip in time really the act of a higher will? The only thing I know for sure is that the experience left us all less righteous in our individual convictions, and at the same time comforted by the feeling that it really didn't matter very much.

GETTING TO KNOW YOU

L ENA forced the issue. She said if I didn't invite her to meet my parents, she'd turn up on their doorstep unannounced and introduce herself. Looking back on it, the surprise attack might have been the better ploy. I was spending the summer at home, working for my father. When I told my mother that my girlfriend was coming for a visit, her face acquired the same flushed, panicked look she got the time I ran in to tell her Dad had fallen off the barn roof and broken his arm.

"Your girlfriend? Visit?" she said.

"This week," I said. "On the weekend. I thought she could stay the night."

"Oh!" she said.

"On the couch," I said.

"The night?" my mother said.

"Louise's old room is too full of junk."

"Overnight?"

"Well, she'll likely take the bus. I thought she could visit longer if she stayed over. You know, get to know everybody."

"This weekend?" said my mother.

"Yes, this weekend. Two days from now. She's coming Saturday."

"We've got to remodel the bathroom!" said my mother.

"Mom!"

"Get your father. We'll move all that stuff out of the bedroom and start wallpapering tonight."

"Mom!"

"Get your father. I need some paint."

"Mom, that's dumb," I said. "It's no big deal."

"We'll have to retile the bathroom," she said.

"No way!" I said. "You don't need to make a big fuss."

My mother took me by the shoulders and looked me in the eye. "Lena can't see mould," she said. "If she sees mould she'll give up on you."

"Mom!"

"Get your father." My mother grabbed pencil and paper and started scribbling. Her eyes glazed over. Her soul was far off. She was in that world only overwhelming panic can create. After a few more tries and no answers I gave up and went to the bathroom. I'd read two *Reader's Digest*s when my father knocked on the door. "Martin?" said my father. "You coming out? I've got to wash up. Your mother wants me to run into town."

"Tonight? It's almost dinnertime. Nothing will be open."

"Camrose. Woolco."

"Yes, Dad."

My father came home with cans of paint, tiles, wallpaper, boxes of bolts and things, a new bathtub and a new bathroom faucet. "Mom," I said. "You're making a big deal out of nothing! A new faucet isn't going to make her love me."

My mother took me by the shoulders for the second time that day and looked me in the eye. "Martin," she said, "listen to me. Try to understand. This is very important. A woman likes a shiny faucet."

I began to suspect a conspiracy to marry me off, to be rid

of me. My family was trying too hard. I left them to it and did the evening chores, and afterwards, in the dying yellow light, I drove my father's tractor and scraper out into the field and dug a slough for the cows in the shape of a heart, and then got the tractor stuck in the muck. I left the tractor where it was and walked down the coulee in the twilight to the deer carcass with the beehive in it, and poked the beehive until the bees swarmed and came after me. When I went into the house to nurse my welts, all that was left of the bathroom was raw plumbing.

"Mom!" I said. She was on her knees with my father, installing the new bathtub.

"I don't want to hear about it," she said.

"This is insane," I said.

"We only want what's best for you," she said.

"You're trying to marry me off," I said. "You want to get rid of me. Don't you?"

"Yes," said my father.

I was wounded. But not that wounded. I went into the kitchen and applied a baking soda and water paste to the bee stings, then made coffee and drank it. I stood in the doorway of the bathroom and watched my folks wallpaper where the mirror used to be. "This is nuts," I said. "Nuts."

"If it makes you feel any better, we're not remodelling the bathroom just for you," said my mother. "I haven't been able to get a shine out of that faucet for years."

I gave up trying to stop my parents and threw myself into the bedroom clean-up. I carried my mother's sewing machine, Louise's stored boxes, my father's beef trophies, and the varnished and framed jigsaw puzzles that were stacked under the bed downstairs to the basement. I stripped Louise's old bed of its bedding, and pulled the bed, mattress and springs out into the living room, and that night

I painted the room a tasteful off-white as my mother instructed. My mother made cocoa at 2:00 A.M. and served it to my father and me at the kitchen table. Her housedress was speckled with paint, and she smelled like the onion she'd put in a bath of water in Louise's old room to get rid of the paint smell. My father's hair had gone suddenly white from the plaster. In a stab that went to my belly, I realized they were growing old. "She better be worth it," said my father.

The Greyhound dropped Lena off in front of the General Store at 9:30 on Saturday morning, and I was there to meet her. This day Lena wore a green dress that was made for a much taller woman, sneakers, her father's bowling jacket and a cap that said "Gainers Meats." At first she had dressed like that so she'd have to be acknowledged for her skills and personality, not what she looked like. Then it just became habit. She really was quite pretty when she smiled, and she did shower regularly and comb her hair; that much I was thankful for. Also, I could hardly complain. I was twenty-three years old and my mother had bought the clothes I had on: a crisp white dress shirt with red plaid jack-shirt over top, jeans, gumboots and a John Deere cap. Lena said she admired me for my lack of style.

"Well," I said. "This is it."

"What?" said Lena.

"This is Likely."

She looked one way and then the other down Centre Avenue. There wasn't much to see, granted, and I wished something marvellous would happen, right there on the street, right then: a car chase, maybe, or a fire. Or a UFO landing. But then St. Paul had the UFO landing pad, built for the centennial celebrations, so a UFO landing on Centre

Avenue was unlikely. Even an earthquake would do. I'd take any happening, just so the town didn't look so bland. It reflected poorly on me.

"How about we look around?" I said.

"That shouldn't take long," said Lena.

The entrepreneurial spirit was alive in Likely. Evangeline Hammerstein had set a sign that said "Sidewalk Sale" in front of Hammerstein's farm equipment dealership. We moseyed over to take a look. About the only things from the dealership on the sale table were three ratty cans of the purple paint Wallace Hammerstein had been trying to get rid of since 1969. The rest was Evangeline's stuff, though it was obvious some of it was her daughter Gudrun's, from Gudrun's two years in university before she'd dropped out; under the tables were several boxes of books and texts no Hammerstein had ever read. On top of the tables was evidence of Evangeline's many attempts at the arts: porcelain piggy banks, three unfinished hooked rugs, several tubes of liquid embroidery paint, a bouquet of fabric flowers, a stack of crocheted doilies and a macramé belt. Lena went straight for the books, and I got interested in a pair of Miss Piggy salt and pepper shakers I thought my mother might like.

One thing that didn't get talked about at Lamentations Church was God's sense of humour. I had never liked it. He seemed to be into practical jokes and was forever tripping me up, like the class bully. Just the night before I'd prayed to him, asking vehemently that during this weekend Lena and I would not run into my relatives, namely Uncle Horace or Uncle George, because inevitably they would embarrass me and knock back my chances of continuing my relationship with Lena. So there she was, fresh off the bus, and who walks out of Hammerstein's dealership but Uncle Horace, and right after him, Uncle George. Ha, ha. Very funny.

I couldn't just ignore them, although that's what Uncle George did to me. He started poking around the sale tables. Horace nodded at me and went straight for the books. I said, "Horace, I'd like to — " But before I'd finished my introduction, he held up his hand and said, "Just a minute, Martin," and went over to Lena and the books. "You just put the guy books to one side there, girlie," he said. "So's I can get at them easy."

"What did you say?" said Lena. I found my interest suddenly drawn to a paint-by-number oil of Elvis, framed lovingly in a gold-enamelled toilet seat.

"Whatever don't interest you, just put them to one side. I hate digging through them romances. Like that one you got in your hand, *Ulysses*, is it? That set in Greece? They'll dress the same romance up and put it any place. But I expect that's what women like. Isn't that so, Martin?"

I grunted ambiguously and picked up a statue of the Virgin Mary decoupaged with Christmas wrap. "I don't know what you're getting at," said Lena.

"Well, it don't matter. Just stack the guy books to one side, will yah?"

Lena jumped up and stuck her face out at Uncle Horace. He took a step back in fright. "I don't know what a guy book is," said Lena. "I don't read romances, and I don't read war books, if that's what you're after. There's no need for gender amongst books. Ever seen two books humping? I haven't. I thought men like you died off with the dinosaurs. Why don't you go dig yourself a hole in Drumheller? What do I look like? A slave? Find your own books, mister."

I saw by my uncle's face that he'd stuck on the word "humping" and hadn't heard a word after. Women in Likely didn't use words like "humping," at least not the Ladies of Lamentations, and they were almost the only women Uncle

Horace had ever come across. He'd looked away as soon as he heard it and made for his truck, forcing Lena to walk behind him if she wanted to finish up her speech. She did. She walked him to his truck and said, "Find your own books" as he started the engine and sped off down the street.

"Who was that guy?" said Lena.

"Have you seen this tea cozy?" I said. "It's made from bottle caps."

Uncle George had been watching all this, of course. He could smell a feminist a mile away, and he never liked the smell. He wandered over to the sale table and came up behind Lena and me. He tapped me on the shoulder. "May I speak with your girlfriend?" he said.

Lena leaped up once again from the box of books, stuck her face into Uncle George's and poked him in the belly. I found renewed interest in the Miss Piggy salt and pepper shakers. "You got something to say to me, you say it to me," said Lena. "Nobody owns me, you understand?"

Uncle George looked at me, looked around to see if Evangeline Hammerstein was watching. She was, so he smiled and fled into the General Store.

"Where'd all these dinosaurs come from?" said Lena.

"That was Uncle George," I said. "Dad's brother."

"Oh," said Lena.

"You might want to go talk to him," I said.

Lena fumbled through the books in the box for a few minutes longer, then, red-faced, marched over to the General Store. Evangeline was looking me over so I smiled and held up the Miss Piggy shakers. "How much?" I said.

After several long minutes Uncle George left the store and stomped over to the Cafe. Lena came back outside and strode up to the sale table and went back to rummaging through the books. "What'd he say?" I said.

"He said a woman should follow her man, but the man should treat his woman with respect and know her wishes. He said the only love that works is married love where the man is the head of the family and God is the head of him. He said he hoped we'd be setting a wedding date soon."

"What'd you say?"

"I said he was full of crap and if you tried to lead me around I'd kick your butt."

"He means well," I said.

Lena dumped the books she'd been handling back into the box. "Nothing here I haven't got," she said. Evangeline rested her arms on her bosom and looked in every direction except towards us.

"I've got to pick up a few things for Mom," I said, and pointed over at the General Store. By then, in 1983, Harry Wyton was dead and the General Store was half the size it used to be; it was divided by a neat white wall, but that's where the renovations stopped. The other half of the store was sometimes a hairdresser, sometimes a craft shop, depending on which one of the Lamentations Ladies was feeling adventuresome. The weekend Lena first came to visit, the other half of the General Store was a day care.

Harry's daughter, Carol Wyton, was sitting behind the counter engrossed in *Love's Wayward Passion*, a paperback. She'd owned and run the store since her father up and died from heartbreak a month after his wife expired of a heart attack. Carol had once competed with my sister, Louise, for the title of Miss Hereford. She wore quite a bit of lipstick and blue eye shadow, and chewed quite a large wad of gum.

Lena picked up a *Leduc Representative* from the newspaper rack, dug out some change from her pocket and went to the counter while I collected items from my mother's shopping list — a bag of screws, a can of mushroom soup and three sheets of sandpaper. Lena cleared her throat. Carol looked up and looked Lena over. She scowled. "You got to pay for that, you know," she said.

Lena held out her handful of change. "I know," she said.

"Well, it's just that the paper's a day late," said Carol. "It's always a day late here."

"That's okay," said Lena.

"I just wanted you to know so you don't get any ideas about not paying. Some people complain. About it being a day late. They buy it and then see it's a day late and then they come back in here and complain."

"It's okay," said Lena. "It doesn't matter."

I came up behind Lena and put a hand on her shoulder. Carol brightened. "This lady's with you?"

"This is Lena," I said, and stood a little straighter. "My girlfriend."

"Well, well. I thought you were just some Calgarian. How come I never heard about this."

"I figured you'd be the first to know," I said. "Carol here knows your business before you do. She's kind of our town crier."

"Well, I've been sick," said Carol. "I haven't been going to the Cafe like I used to. You know how it is when you run a business."

I nodded sympathetically. Lena counted out her coins and put them on the counter.

"No, no, dear, that's okay," said Carol. "We're always a day late here anyway. Hardly seems right to charge."

We were outside the store, on the way to my father's pickup, when Lena dropped the bombshell. "My parents are coming tonight," she said.

"Parents?"

"I would have come with them, but I thought I'd better

warn you. They want to meet your mom and dad. I said it wasn't a good idea, but there's no telling Mom anything. She came up with an excuse about stopping in on their way to Edmonton. Suddenly she's got to visit Auntie Phyllis. She hasn't talked to Auntie Phyllis since Auntie Phyllis tried to pinch my father's butt at the Farmers' Institute dance."

I didn't so much fear meeting Lena's parents — what's more stress when you're already stressed? But I did fear my mother's reaction, given what she had done in response to the news Lena was coming for a visit. My mother was on the doorstep when Lena and I drove into the yard. She was dressed in her Sunday best and was momentarily taken aback by Lena's green dress, sneakers and bowling jacket, but she had restored her smile by the time we reached the door. My mother shook Lena's hand and slapped her on the shoulder. "Lena, it's so good to finally meet you," she said.

"I'm very happy to meet you, Mrs. Winkle," said Lena.

"Elsie, call me Elsie."

Introductions and pleasantries over with, my mother, Lena and I settled into coffee and cookies. Dad was still out feeding the cattle. I thought I'd make Lena's parents' visit sound like a casual thing, old friends dropping in. "By the way," I said. "Lena's folks are popping in for coffee this evening."

"Lena's folks?" said my mother.

"They're dropping in on their way to Edmonton," I said. "They're visiting Lena's aunt."

"Tonight?"

"I brought you these," I said, and held out the Miss Piggy shakers. My mother took them and stared at them for a few moments. Lena took off her Gainers Meats cap and put it on again.

"Well, what's more company when the house is full," said Mom.

"Full? What do you mean?"

"I invited Marion and Horace and George and Gilda over. They wanted to meet Lena."

"Not Uncle Horace," I said.

"I've already invited them," said Mom. "There's no way around it."

"I'm sorry to be so much trouble," said Lena.

"You've been no trouble at all," said Mom.

That night Uncle Horace and Aunt Marion and Uncle George and Aunt Gilda all turned up at once, which was something of a problem because it meant they had already traded notes on Lena and all that had gone on that morning. Lena and I watched them drive up and park. She pointed at Uncle Horace. "That's the other dinosaur," said Lena.

"Yup," I said.

"He's your uncle too?"

"Yup."

"I've got things off on the wrong foot," said Lena.

"Well," I said.

"No, I'm sorry. I'll make it up to you. I'll be on my best behaviour. I'll be downright cheerful. I'll charm their pants off."

I was about to suggest that this might not be the best approach, either, when Uncle Horace and Aunt Marion and Uncle George and Aunt Gilda all piled in through the front door. There are many contradictions in the community of Likely. One is that while young men with long hair are not only frowned on but denied jobs, old balding men grow their hair as long as they can, at least on one side, and then they comb the long hair sideways over their bald spots. This was Uncle Horace's hairdo. Uncle George, on the other hand, had gone out and bought himself a toupee, which everyone thought was just plain prideful, but you don't tell Uncle George a thing like that. Toupees were only tolerated on men like Pastor Gottlieb, men in the public eye with positions of authority. For Uncle George to wear a toupee was presumptuous. Everybody blamed it on that year he had spent in Edmonton, and my parents feared much worse might happen to me before I completed my studies there.

The year in Edmonton had left its scars on Aunt Gilda as well. That night she wore a bright pink dress opened right down to the third button, and lipstick and blue eye shadow. Worse, she was downright outgoing.

"This is Lena," I said. "Aunt Marion, and I believe you remember Horace. This is Uncle George, of course, and Aunt Gilda."

"It's so good to meet you!" said Aunt Marion, and before I could warn Lena not to, she had my Aunt Marion in a hug and was heading in Uncle Horace's direction. Aunt Marion looked a little dazed and then regained herself and smiled. Uncle Horace took a step back into the closet, knocking over the brooms and boots. In the fuss of Mom running over to pick up the brooms and Aunt Marion apologizing, Horace managed to avoid the hug completely. Lena stood there looking uncertain until Aunt Gilda, who was well versed in hugs, having done some therapy, hugged Lena. Uncle George just sat himself down at the kitchen table, avoided all attempts at eye contact and said nothing. In fact he said almost nothing all night, which was probably for the best.

"I understand you study plants," said Marion.

"Weeds," said Lena.

"Fascinating," said Marion.

"Sit! Sit!" said my mother. We all sat around the kitchen table except my mother. She served us coffee, tea and five kinds of squares. Several days of panic had settled into my mother as a kind of euphoria. She had gone beyond the need for sleep or rest or even food. She ran on coffee and tea, and was no longer able to sit down for lengths greater than one minute. Instead she found reasons to clank around the kitchen. We all listened to my mother clank. Aunt Gilda and Aunt Marion smiled at Lena and snuck looks at her clothes — Lena had changed into a black skirt that reached the floor, a T-shirt that said "Sue Me" and a pair of bowling shoes for the occasion — and then asked, again, if they could do anything to help. My mother said, "No," a little more shrilly each time. My father stretched his legs and put his hands in his pockets, Uncle George sulked, Uncle Horace scratched his crotch, and I fumbled with Lena's hand. I had been struck dumb by this event, and I began to have an understanding of my father's many silences. Aunt Gilda and Marion smiled. Lena smiled back. We waited.

When the Henklemans finally drove into the yard, my family, except Uncle George, all leaped up and ran to the door to greet them. Mr. Henkleman wore a cap that said "Old Fart" and he didn't take it off when he and Mrs. Henkleman came in and sat at the table with Uncle George and the rest of us. My mother kept looking at the cap as she poured more tea and coffee. Mr. Henkleman saw her looking and pointed at his hat. "Pretty good, eh?" he said and nudged Mrs. Henkleman. "Lorna here picked it up for me. Suits me, eh?"

My mother blanched and looked away. "Fart's a bit of a swear word in these parts," I said.

"Martin," my mother said quietly.

"Oh, fart's a wonderful word," said Lena. "Did you know fart goes all the way back to the Anglo-Saxons? Fart's one of the very few words an Anglo-Saxon farmer of a thousand years ago would understand. That and tits."

"Lena!" said Mrs. Henkleman.

"Well, teats ain't a swear word around here," said Uncle Horace. "Got too many of them around, eh? On the cows."

"Tits, dear, not teats," said Marion. "Sorry, his hearing's been going lately."

"Speaking of that," said Uncle Horace. "I went into Hammerstein's for a part this morning, at nine o'clock on the button. Nine o'clock. It says the hours right on the door, 8:30 A.M. to 5:00 P.M., and the door's locked. That's pretty shoddy business."

"There's a law about that," said Uncle George. "You got to open when you say you're going to open. In fact, there's a standard. Banks got to open at 9:00. Hardware stores at 8:30. Restaurants at 7:00 A.M."

"Where'd you get that from?" said Aunt Gilda.

"Read it somewhere," said Uncle George.

"That's just foolishness," said Mrs. Henkleman. "A business is the owner's business. They can open and close when they please. If you've got to close the shop for some reason, like a funeral, say, then you go ahead and close it. There's no law about it."

We all watched Uncle George go further into his sulk. The room went silent for a minute. "Well, a funeral's different," said Dad, finally. "In my father's day a town closed down for a funeral. Every shop closed and the owners went to the funeral. That was community."

My mother put down a plate of her famous butterscotch squares. "Look at these!" said Uncle Horace, and he grabbed one, put it in his mouth and talked with his mouth full. "We were over visiting Marion's niece the other day and she put store-bought cookies down on the table. Imagine! Store-bought!"

"Then she said, 'I don't bake any more,' as if she was proud of it!" added Aunt Marion.

"I've never even baked a cookie," said Lena.

Uncle Horace and Aunt Marion, Uncle George and Aunt Gilda, my mother and father all looked away in horror. In Likely a good deal of a woman's worth is weighted on the tastiness of her squares, just as a man is judged on his ability to work a fifteen-hour day out in the fields when necessary. Each lady in the Ladies of Lamentations church group guarded her particular recipe for squares as some small countries guard their national treasures. Even my sister, Louise, didn't know my mother's recipe for butterscotch squares, although Louise made a pretty good square of her own. Lena had other talents — she was destined to work for the government finding new ways to kill weeds — but I still felt ashamed.

"I don't see the big deal," said Lena. "I don't have time to bake. Don't much like it even if I had the time. I've got better things to do."

There was another long silence, and then my mother stood. "Well," she said. "How about some more tea?"

Later that night, after everyone had left, I took Lena for a walk through the pasture in the moonlight. "I think it went pretty well," I said.

"They don't know what to make of me," said Lena. "They think I'm a freak."

"They thought Pierre Trudeau was a freak," I said. "They just need to get used to you."

"I keep catching your dad looking at my clothes," said Lena.

I looked down at the ruffled hem of her skirt and the slip that showed over her bowling shoes. "You dress a little different from what folks around here are used to," I said.

"You don't like the way I dress?"

"I never said that," I said, and when that didn't seem like enough I said, "You're beautiful in whatever you wear."

I took Lena by the hand and showed her the slough I'd dug in the shape of a heart. "I made this for you," I said.

"Oh, Martin," said Lena. We sat in the tractor beside the heart-shaped slough, surrounded by my father's cattle, and kissed.

When we came back into the house, my mother had two cups of cocoa ready and bedding on the couch. The paint fumes in Louise's old room were still overpowering. My father was already in bed, reading a book. Lena and I drank our cocoas slowly, at opposite ends of the table where my mother had positioned our cups, and waited for my mother to quit fussing around in the kitchen and go to bed. But we couldn't outwait my mother. The cocoa didn't last long enough. We both rose. "Bedtime?" said my mother. We nodded. She took Lena's hand and stuffed a scrap of paper into it.

"What's this?" said Lena.

My mother smiled and patted Lena's hand. "It's my recipe for butterscotch squares."

I knew by the look on Lena's face, after we'd kissed goodnight in front of my mother, that Lena expected me to come to her in the night. But I couldn't. I lay in bed stiff, metaphorically, as a board, torn between the heaviness of a lifetime of moral training and my lover's expectations. Yet I knew also that if I waited long enough, Lena would come to me.

Then I realized if Lena tried to traverse the basement stairs down to my room, in the dark, through the junk I'd piled there, the outcome could be fatal. Lena would trip over my sister's box of childhood knickknacks, sending the bicycles and my father's beef trophies flying. The noise would wake my mother and my mother would kill us both for sure.

I wrapped myself in the drab blue quilt my mother had made for me in 1971 from several of my father's old Sunday shirts and crept up the stairs. As it turned out, Lena respected my mother's house rules and didn't attempt to come to me in the night after all. In the morning my mother found me sitting at the head of the stairs. "Martin, what are you doing here?" she said.

"Couldn't sleep," I said.

"You were snoring," she said.

"I couldn't sleep and I was on my way upstairs for some milk, and then suddenly I got so tired I had to sit down and then I fell asleep. It must be all that midnight redecorating."

"Isn't that funny," said my mother. "The same thing happened to me just yesterday when I went to get a jar of peaches from the cold room. It's been some week."

"Yes," I said.

"Well, we better get ourselves dressed for church," said Mom.

"Ah, I'm taking Lena up to Tofield this morning," I said.

"I thought you were coming to church with us," said Mom.

"I never said we were going to church," I said.

"I just thought," said my mother. "Anyway, everyone's expecting you."

Lena stuck her head around the stair doorway and looked down at me. "It's okay," she said. "We can go."

"But," I said.

"It'll be good," said Lena. "It'll give me a perspective on you."

That was exactly what I was afraid of.

We dressed — Lena in harem pants, a beaded top and one of my work shirts, my mother in her best blue Sunday dress, and my father and I both in white shirts and black dress pants. All four of us squeezed into my father's pickup. I sat through the service with sweating palms and thudding heart and a knot in my neck the size of an orange. Then came the moment I had been dreading. Pastor Gottlieb shot a smile at me so big and welcoming I wanted to run outside and hide in the Ford. "Oh God, they're going to make us stand," I whispered.

"What?" said Lena.

"I hear we've got a guest among us," said Pastor Gottlieb. "Stand up there for us, Martin, and introduce your friend. Stand up, Lena. Let's welcome Lena, everyone. Lena… Henkleman? Yes, Henkleman. From Vulcan."

Dutifully we stood. I grabbed Lena's hand in panic and squeezed it and fumbled with it and tried to fit a smile on my face. I realized I wasn't sure just how, at that moment, a smile went. Lena pulled her hand from my sweaty, painful grip and patted me so I'd sit down again. We sat.

"Be prepared for after," I said.

"After?"

"After the service," I said.

At Pastor Gottlieb's last amen we were mobbed. The faces I'd known all these years took on a different quality. I saw them through Lena's eyes, or at least I thought I did. They were an odd, ragtag group of people. They'd suddenly got old and I'd missed it somehow. Wallace Hammerstein was bumped this way and that as he tried to work his way into the group to shake Lena's hand. Bierlie was more tottery on his fake leg than I'd ever seen him before. Lindskoog was Lindskoog, though he was fragile now, paler. Someone brought Lena a cup of coffee. There were several invitations for lunch. I took up a post near the coffee maker and watched Lena in the midst of the mob. She saw me watching her and pulled an ape face.

There is something about Lena that makes me want to break the rules. All of a sudden I wanted to kiss her, there, in that church. And you know what? I did. I took her hand, pulled her out of the crowd to the doorway of the church and kissed her. In front of all those people, I kissed her. It was no big act of rebellion, but it was enough to make Lena grin and enough to put smiles on the judging faces of my past; enough to make me feel suddenly and finally at home.